Roots and Branches

by
Marcus A. White

authorHOUSE

AuthorHouse™
1663 Liberty Drive, Suite 200
Bloomington, IN 47403
www.authorhouse.com
Phone: 1-800-839-8640

© *2008 Marcus A. White. All rights reserved.*

No part of this book may be reproduced, stored in a retrieval system, or transmitted by any means without the written permission of the author.

First published by AuthorHouse 9/15/2008

ISBN: 978-1-4389-1093-2 (sc)

Printed in the United States of America
Bloomington, Indiana

This book is printed on acid-free paper.

Cover illustration and design by Gabrielle L. Jolly.
Contact the author at marcuswhite@verizon.net

Dying without trying is not living at all.

-Marcus A. White

1

"Donald "Duck" Matthews will be a great writer once he has suffered more."
-Robert Townsend, The Five Heartbeats (1991)

Life has taught me that I have some anti-social/anxiety issues now. I feel very uncomfortable when talking to people. My heart races and it's like my tongue is too big, I can't breathe right and I am not pronouncing my words correctly. I get this feeling even when talking to people that I love. But the release of my first book has forced me to become more of a social butterfly. I have to do a lot of one on one talking now. The main reason for that is because daily I am asked questions relating to my book. Personal questions. The types that are always followed by the offerings of ones own personal situations that only feel right when spoken quietly and in private. Also since I released my first book I have found that there are a lot of ambivalent writers out there. The *"Almost Authors"* who start writing a book and then put it on the shelf until the spirit moves them to pick it up again. *"I have been working on this idea for a children's book for years and can't find the time to finish it."* I have also learned there are lots of mothers with children in the pen. A lot. I kind of appreciate them the most. Even though I'm still in the hood grinding it out, they make me feel like I am different, like I made it. If that makes any sense. *"I wish you could talk to my son. I'm going to send him a copy of your book. I think it will help him."* I get that a lot and I wonder why that is? I find that funny because I have a hard time seeing where my story is helpful. I think that it may be because I give off the impression that I am doing fine. I work hard at pretending. That is probably why I hate talking to people. Maybe I'm afraid they can tell. I try to be nice and respectful, keep a job and do right by my children but I know the monster is still there lurking.

The one question that I am asked far more than any other is, *"When are you going to write another book?"* I love that question because it gives me a feeling of creditability and every time it is asked I think to myself, *"If they want more then I must not be too bad of a writer."* I always say, *"I'm working on it."* Which isn't a total lie. I have always been *"working"* on my next book ever since I saw the first one with my name on the cover. (What a big moment for me that was.) At least mentally I have been working on it. I have thoroughly enjoyed the success of my first book so much that everyday I hope to have a thought or two that will lead to my next book. I hate to say success because it hasn't blown up yet but from the responses that I have received, I feel that there are not too many degrees of separation from my book and total success. I have to believe that, otherwise what's the use? So far my book has allowed me to receive letters of encouragement with words of support and enlightenment from Nikki Giovanni and Tavis Smiley as well as a 5-star review on Borders.com.

The 5-star review came from an unlikely source. I was on my way to work one morning and found that the Green Line of the metro was shut down. I decided to U it up at the station and head back home. I got on the A4 Bus and sat next to, of all things in Anacostia, a white man. I noticed he was reading a magazine, so I hesitantly asked him if he was a big reader. He said that he wasn't really but that his wife was. So I told him about my book and gave him a post card with all the book information on it. He told me that he would get his wife to read my book and write a review on it. As the bus made its way through the hood, I sat next to this guy and just had a normal conversation. It was different. At one point I told him that I was really curious to know what white people would think of my book. His reply gave me a little insight into his personality. He said, *"Well, I know some white people. In fact, my best friend is a white person."* I bet he is a funny guy. In his five-star review of my book, my new white friend Leo said that my prose was not pretty but it was engaging. He also said that my book seemed to lose focus and became disconnected at the end. I agree wholeheartedly with his assessment and because of that review I plan to finish this book strong. *Learn from your mistakes.*

My first book was born out of boredom. I worked a job that allowed me ample time to clickety-clack on the computer. And on top of that I was really angry and depressed and had a story to tell. Now what? What do I write about? I thought about the things that I have problems with and opinions on in this world. Religion. Government. Child Support Enforcement. The list could go on, believe me. But then I took a step back and decided to just write. Go with the flow. This book is going to be my version of *"Roc Live."* There will be no paper trail of book worthy ideas and phrases scribbled on post-it notes and long yellow pages to accumulate on my dining room table. This book will be a direct-connect from my brain to the computer. As I sit here on my balcony typing away, I have no idea what is coming next. I don't just mean the next chapter. I mean the next sentence. I wonder where it will end up. As I sit here now I wonder if the good guy wins in the end.

I've been told that the quotes I used in my first book were a really good addition and I received a lot of really nice comments on them. My readers seemed to like how each quote foreshadowed the chapters. So I thought I would try it again and attempt to use the quotes as a signature of a Marcus White work. I hope that's playing fair because I haven't yet figured out my writing style and process and I kind of need the quotes to help me get started from time to time. I learned that from Finding Forrester. Sean Connery suggested that young kid, Jamal, start his writing assignments off with the first line of someone else's work and let those words jump-start and lead him. I totally understand what he was trying to teach the kid. Sometimes I need that little boost myself. Starting a chapter is the hardest. That first paragraph of a new one is always a pain in the brain, believe me. Therefore, I chose the first quote of my new book very carefully as I will all the quotes that I use in this book.

I used to be a big movie guy and I absolutely loved The Five Heartbeats because *"Can't nobody sang like Eddie Kane Jr.☺"* But really, sometimes words and phrases in certain scenes speak to me. This one did. For some reason that scene of Robert Townsend standing on that stage, mad at his girl and J.T., stuck with me. Just like the one in The Color Purple where Miss Sophia had to leave her family on Christmas Day because the white lady couldn't get the car to act right and the scene from Glory, where Denzel spoke to the men as they sat around the campfire singing hymns and mentally preparing for battle. Entrancing scenes in Marcus White's Memory Movie Database for sure but the main reason that I selected the Five Heartbeats quote, over any other, to start my new book off is because I want to see if it is true in theory.

"Marcus White will be a great writer once he has suffered more."

Through much fault of my own, I am separated from my daughters, my babies that I love more than anything else in this whole world and now have to share them with any Jake their mother decides to bring home. For a father like me, one who adores his children; this is suffering at its worse. So let's see if Donald *"Duck"* Matthews knew what the hell he was talking about.

2

> *"...Fame is the worst drug known to man. It's stronger than heroin when u can look in the mirror like there I am. And still not see what you've become. I know I'm guilty of it too but not like them."*
>
> -Jay Z, Kingdom Come (2007)

When the kids come over to my house whatever is missing is usually found on the floor somewhere. So when I walked into the kitchen one day and saw a Topps trading card on the floor, I thought nothing of it and just bent down, as usual, to pick it up. When I turned it over and saw that it had Jay-Z's picture on it, I stopped for a second and thought, *"Damn, Jay-Z is actually on a Topps trading card. This man is large."* The man is a personal motivation to me and a lot of the time when I daydream about my future, he is at my side. Therefore, I felt it was disrespectful to leave the card on the floor or throw it away. It was sort of like finding a Bible on the floor. Whether you are religious or not, you can't leave a Bible on the floor. It's just wrong. So I grabbed one of the kid's magnets and placed the Jay-Z card on the refrigerator, right at eye level, to use as a reminder when I feel the road is too long. A reminder that if he can make it then so can I.

From the bottom to the top...

I am a visionary of sorts and some might call the feelings that I have delusions of grandeur or pipe dreams even. But I feel a necessity to make it big in life and simply call the feelings I've always had a refusal to be ordinary. For many years I have been addicted to that drug Jay-Z was rapping about and I am hoping that my writing finally gets that monkey off my back. If I were to write that song from the quote above, I would have to end that line with, *"I know I'm guilty of it too just like them."* That's because every morning I walk into the bathroom and see *"Failure"* scrawled across the mirror in bright red lipstick. I just haven't been able to figure out whose handwriting it is in yet. I sure hope it is not my mother's.

I am a published author. That alone should cause some sort of spike in my ego palpitations. But no, nothing. I still feel like plain old Marc. With the publishing of my first book I have received so much praise. Way more praise than I ever expected. And always, as I stand there in the presence of the individual telling me how wonderful they find my book to be, I feel unworthy. I have never been one to pat myself on the back. No one is harder on me than me. That is fact. I believe that everyone has a life that is book worthy. Whether the life is filled with joy and pain or sunshine and rain, there is still a story there. Who doesn't have memories?

I was telling a lady at work about my family's reaction to my first book being published. I told her how excited and proud of me they all were and how siced they were to see their names in print. Then I told her how hard it was for me to see the big deal that they all made about it. Her response was a motherly, *"Aww, you are still humble."* Her comment made me think about why I feel the way I do about my book. I came to the conclusion that it isn't a question of humility versus overconfidence as much as it is an aversion to my personal opinion of myself. Or should I say my *selves*? I feel like three people. The first I want to be. The second concerns me a little. The third is just plain frightening.

Marcus White. You would be proud to have this guy date your daughter. He's a very proud father and even a published author. He holds open the door for elderly ladies and gives up his seat to women with babies. He makes sure that his kids have what they want and what they need and gives away computer services usually for free. He always wears his seatbelt tight and doesn't cross the street without having the light. He takes pride in his work and he loved his mother so. He sits down in front of a computer screen and lets his memory flow. Wiping out the demons of his past with each and every paragraph. Hoping one day to look back and laugh on all the bad things that came to pass.

Marcus Gray. This guy is cloudy, blurry and hard to make sense. He straddles the line and lives on the fence. He creeps back and forth into the realms of Good and Bad, a sine wave resembles his path. Your left is his right. Your right is his wrong. It seems no one can figure his ass. By hook or by crook is okay with him, as he feels there are varying degrees of sin. He makes his way by any means necessary because he is so determined to win. A little too determined at times? I would guess, maybe. And there are times when he feels some regret. But if crossing the line gets him to the church on time then regrets he one day will forget.

Marcus Black. He's secretive and he's shady. I don't know what else I can say about him except when he's backed into a corner he'll make a move on a whim. He is a homegrown insurgent and enemy of the state. Illegal or sanctified he feels all means are justified to keep food on his children's plate. He drives dirty with no license and falsified tags putting it all on the line with only a quarter tank of gas. Ducking through alleyways dodging the feds, he cuts corners like Swiss cheese and loaves of white bread. Time after time he blindly ignores the signs, willingly sacrificing everything trying to turn nickels into dimes.

Signs. They are everywhere. I'm not talking about bridge-closed warnings, stop and yield or any other traffic related signs. I'm talking about the signs that can change your life if you miss or catch them. The people that pay attention to them are the ones that avoid disaster.

I've learned that. The first night that you sit there in a jail cell knowing you are not going home any time soon, you think about all the signs that you ignored before your capture. *"Something told me to put the coke outside. I saw that car creepin' through twice today, I knew something wasn't right."* I have ignored thousands of signs that cost me thousands of hours of pain and confinement.

I finally had a sign that was impossible to ignore.

A good friend at work told me once that my first book didn't make prison sound scary. I told her what I tell everyone else and that is that the most frightening part of my prison experience was getting released. The horrors that I thought I would face, when I was inside dying to get out, paled in comparison to the monsters that I encountered upon my release. When I came home from prison it didn't take me long to see that the people with whom I had to play The Game with simply did not play fair. It wasn't a quick decision but I decided that if I had to step off the path from time to time when all else failed then oh well. A quick move here or a good deal there were the only things that kept my furniture off the curb sometimes. I'm not perfect and never claimed to be but that way of thinking was always an option. It is something that gets embedded deep within you and is so hard to get rid of. I would slip onto the *"dark side"* and be back in the light, quietly passing my peers like two ships in the night, before anyone knew I was missing. But it was stressful, very stressful. Doing dirt always is.

A phone call, actually the sight of several phone calls finally changed that way of thinking for me. I came home from work and saw my cousin Poogie's number on the Caller-Id several times. And the calls were placed at times of the day when he would have known that I was at work. To me, that screamed desperation. Seeing his number on the phone like that scared the hell out of me. It brought back those memories of death notifications in the middle of the night. I knew something was wrong. He could have been calling to tell me about his mother coming up from North Carolina or one of his son Blake's football games but I felt the tension build up inside of me. *"I have been here before. I know this feeling."* I knew it was something bad. I hesitantly called him back. The first words out of his mouth were, *"They got Lee, Marc."* My first question was, *"Who got him?"* He was like, *"The Feds."* That's when it really hit me. Lee had always sold *"something"* so we all knew that jail was a step away for him at all times but this wasn't some county or state charge. This was federal. And the Feds don't come get you until they got you. Lee was basically cooked and it was making me sick. I sat down and thought about his girl and their kids. I thought about the house that they just got together and worried about how Tika was going to handle everything without him. Then I thought about me. There comes a time in every man's life when he gets to a point where he says enough is enough. As you get older, have children, buy houses and stuff, the risks of unsafe activities become too great. Lee was always a fallback plan for me. Forrest Gump said, *"Sometimes I guess there just aren't enough rocks."* In my case, the rocks were dollars and when there weren't enough I always knew that I could go to Lee. One way or another he always made sure I had what I needed or what I needed to get what I needed and I know I wasn't the only one that kept him as an ace in the hole. There were many people that relied on him for help. Not just me. That is why I try to do what I can for his family while he is away as I know he would do and has done the same if I were in his place or a place just as bad. I believe that Lee's desire to be a provider to all of us was one of the reasons that made him continue down his path without flinching. Technology has made selling drugs a lot harder than it used to be and Lee knew that but hustling was all he really knew and it rewarded him so well. So it wasn't a question of how could he stop doing what he was doing? The question was always, *"Why should he stop doing what he was doing?"*

I hate to speak of Lee in the past tense but he is a 40-year-old three-time loser facing 5 to 15 years fed time, so the past tense seems to fit here. By the way, three-time loser is a prison reference that means he has been in the system three different times not that I think of my good friend as a loser. He is very important to me and I tend to look at his latest incarceration selfishly. If nothing else good comes out of it, at least I recognized the sign that was unwittingly forced upon me and promised myself from the moment I hung up the phone to go completely straight. So nowadays, when I am asked, *"Marc what you got?"* I take pride in saying, *"I don't have nothing. I'm out of The Game, Joe."* I take pride because so many of us didn't make it out. Ask Lee. Thanks to the F.B.I, I now have no fallback plan and I am on the fence about it. On one hand I am happy that I finally see err in my ways and welcome the challenge of becoming legally successful. On the other hand I am sick about losing Lee, one of my best friends ever, in order to have my eyes finally opened.

My memory and my fingers are my fallback plan now because Lee is out of the picture and more. If it's going to be done then it's on me to be the one, to close that prison door for sure. Life forced me to keep it open as an option from time to time but now my options are more limited, so I have to sell books like I used to sell dimes. The wants that I desire, fame and critical acclaim, will not be attained by playing the Drug Game. They will have to come through my writing. They will have to come from my pain.

3

"Daddy, I flew in a helicopter."
-Deja Celene White

Sometimes I think I am the only person in the city that doesn't own a cell phone. I see kids, drunks and people that I know don't have any money, walking around with them. In this day and age not having one is like saying, *"I don't have an email address"* or *"I've never heard of American Idol."* But for me, most of the worst days in my life started with the ringing of a telephone. I know that's why I hate them so much.

When the phone rang early one January morning in 2003 to inform me that my two daughters and their mother were involved in a car accident on I-95 with a tractor-trailer, I almost lost it. Through the phone, I could hear one of my babies crying in the background. I rushed out of the house like a madman and sped to the scene. It was the same route I took after I found out my mama died. I was scared shitless.

The accident happened when Chrisi swerved to avoid a tractor-trailer that came into her lane, lost control of her truck and slammed into the jersey wall. She had a cut on her forehead that was bleeding and was almost in a total panic. I could see the fear on her face and in the way she moved. I remember feeling sorry for her and for what she must have been feeling. Looking back on that day I wish I had given her a hug. I know she needed one. Desiree, who was five at the time, had a strawberry-sized abrasion on her face and her leg was sore. Her big pretty eyes were as wide as those of a deer when caught in a vehicle's headlights.

Deja said, *"Daddy, my stomach hurts."*

The scene was one that I witnessed personally time and time again. Traffic backed up, ambulances and fire engines were pulling up, sirens blaring and emergency personnel scurrying all around. I have driven past many accident scenes in my time but this is one that I will never forget because my babies were right in the middle of it.

They were all rushed to the hospital by ambulance. By the time I got there the three of them were back in a room that was filled with nurses and doctors running in and out. I knew from the frantic pace of moment that it was serious. I also knew that if I lost it then Chrisi would really lose it. So I used everything in me to look and act assured that everything was going to be fine, even though inside I was trembling with fear and wrestling with the fact that my baby was not all right.

There was something wrong with Deja's stomach.

Every time a doctor or nurse would touch her abdomen, she would cry out in pain. The kids were eating those orange Lance cheese and crackers when they had the accident. I remembered seeing them strewn all about the back seat of the truck when I got to the accident scene. Now she was vomiting them all over the floor. I was watching my baby suffer and it was killing me. They wanted to perform an MRI on her to see what was causing the pain. First, she had to drink this contrast liquid in order for them to see the problem with her stomach. It was pink, thick and I'm sure tasted awful. I don't remember the exact amount that she was supposed to drink before they could begin the MRI but whatever it was she never got close. When they saw that she could not drink it by herself, they attempted to get it down themselves, almost forcing it at times but it always came squirting back up. It seemed like as soon as she got it down it would spew out all over the place. My baby was gagging, puking and covered in mess. I felt helpless but didn't pray.

After what seemed like a lifetime of trying unsuccessfully to get her to keep the liquid down, the doctors finally decided to proceed with the MRI. I held her hand tightly as they wheeled her into room. Maybe a little too tightly for a six-year-old but my baby wasn't leaving me.

The noise of the MRI frightened her and lying flat on the board caused my baby to suffer through some excruciating pain. I know that because I saw her eyes and heard her make sounds that six-year-olds shouldn't. I tried to convince her to stay still. Stillness though, was impossible because all children know is that they hurt.

After the MRI, the four of us waited in the room for the results. Chrisi was a wreck; she saw the words *"possible death"* handwritten on a sheet of paper with our baby's name on it. That basically took her completely out of the game. I continued to conceal my real feelings of dread and worry and went about trying to make everyone believe that we were going to be okay. I was worried about Desiree witnessing all of this, so I called my Aunt Phyl to come get her. She was there in what seemed like an instant. Family.

With Desiree shaken and stirred but safe, Chrisi and I could now focus solely on Deja. I didn't let the thought of Deja dying stay on my mind. Not even when Chrisi told me about what she saw on the paper. I brushed it off almost as if it were just a formality and something they had to write down in order to cover all hospital bases. *"My baby is not going to die. Are you kidding me?"* The doctor poked his head in and he called Chrisi and me outside the room for the news. This is a Marcus White book so of course the news was not good.

Deja's pancreas was severed. She was bleeding internally. Whoa.

She required way more attention than the local hospital could give. What she required was emergency surgery. Immediately. We must have signed our names a million times on a million forms as we watched what seemed like a million doctors and nurses strap our baby up on a gurney. They wheeled her out of the emergency room and told us to meet her at Children's Hospital in Washington. We kissed her and told her everything was going to be okay and headed out of the hospital.

"I'm leaving on a jet plane. I don't know if I'll be back again."

Up... up... and away. She left us but not on a jet plane. Instead, she left in a bright yellow med-evac helicopter headed to the city. Chrisi and I watched from the front seats of my truck as the rotors spun up on the chopper with our baby inside. As it took off I could no longer hold in the pain and gave up the fight. I mean that wasn't just any little girl flying off to the city with strangers, it was Daddy's little girl. I was a mess. And just like I knew would happen if I lost it, Chrisi followed suit. We sat there for a few minutes together, crying in disbelief that this was happening and scared to death that we might lose our child.

My first impression of The Children's Hospital of Washington was based solely on the outside of the building. I didn't like the black windows and thought it was an architectural disaster. Whoever said that you shouldn't judge a book by its cover must have been talking about this hospital. I say that because inside its oddly bubbled façade, The Children's Hospital of Washington is packed full of the best doctors and staff in the world. The best. No question.

Deja was taken straight from the helicopter and prepared for surgery. When we got there she was just about to be taken back to the operating room. We got to spend a minute with her in the hallway before they wheeled her away. There was a strong possibility that it would be one of those *"last goodbyes"* but it didn't feel like it at all. I was shocked at how calm she was. She didn't seem to be in any pain and was almost giddy about the helicopter flight. She smiled. I needed to see that and I silently hoped that it was not the last one that I would witness.

I am killing myself trying to remember how we passed the time during the surgery. I am sure there were several phone calls made and millions of prayers prayed but try as I might, I can't pull those few hours out of my memory.

After an eternity of worry and fear, the doctor came out to see us. The surgery was a success. There was a sudden feeling of relief that came over me that is hard to explain in words but as always with me, I saw a similar feeling very well captured once in a movie. The movie was *Man on Fire* and at the end of it Denzel was all shot up and walking across the bridge to meet the kidnappers.

I spent the first half of the movie watching Denzel fall in love with this little cute white girl. Sometimes it was hard to discern if the love between the two of them was genuine or just Hollywood. Either way it is a great Dad movie. The little girl was kidnapped and supposedly killed. Hearing this devastated and enraged Denzel. Therefore, he would spend the next half of the movie on an unforgiving war party that was direct, brutal, relentless and merciless. Honestly it was like watching love kill. After his rampage he found evidence that the little girl might still be alive. To make a great long story short he ends up on the bridge to meet the kidnappers and make a trade for the girl. On the phone, the kidnapper told him, *"I give you her life for your life."* Denzel agreed without hesitation, hung up the phone and headed to the bridge.

This is where I saw the feeling that I felt in the hospital after finding out Deja was going to be fine. As Denzel is dragging himself across the bridge, he sees the car door open and out pops the little girl, Pita. It was not a hoax. She was really alive. He breathed a sigh filled with so much relief that it puffed up his cheeks like he was blowing out candles on a birthday cake. That is as close to describing how I felt as I can get it. I guess you have to see the movie or face the possibility of the death of your child in order to really know.

We were allowed to see Deja shortly after speaking with the doctor. She was in the PICU, Pediatric Intensive Care Unit and looked just like children look in their parent's worst nightmares. She had this huge brace on her neck and all types of cables and wires connected to one or another piece of equipment that were all beeping and dripping. Her little arm was filled with needles, gauze and tape and to top it off she had a six-inch incision running vertically down her stomach from the bottom of her sternum to just above her belly button. The initial sight of it made me feel so sorry for her. *"Aww, my poor baby."* She was still heavily sedated, so she couldn't talk to us. We just stood there and looked at her.

We wanted to stay there by her side but there are no sleep accommodations available for parents in the PICU. It was a long day. We had been in one hospital or another since early in the morning. It was about 9:30PM or so when we decided to go home for the night, rest as best we could and planned to head back to the hospital first thing in the morning. I remember when we got to the house we just flopped down on the sofa. Chrisi said, *"Marc, is Deja gonna be all right?"* Naturally I said, *"Yes."* Then we sat quietly and tried to take in the immensity of the day's events. That took all of about ten minutes because the next thing I know, we were in my truck headed back to the hospital. We couldn't leave her there alone. After all that she had been through, we needed to be there with her even if she didn't know we were there.

One thing I learned about The Children's Hospital of Washington is that they are always packed. We had been on a roller coaster ride of emotional ups and downs since early in the morning. Our tanks were way past empty. We were drained physically and spiritually and we desperately needed sleep. Tomorrow would come early and require full awareness so rest was a must. We searched through all the waiting rooms looking for somewhere to sleep. They were all full of sleepy and worried parents. We finally found a hard, cold and quiet spot on the floor of a common area. Well it was quiet, at least until we were startled awake by the squelching of a security guard's radio. Seems we couldn't sleep there. I am guessing that we made the first of our one thousand trips to the snack machine because I don't remember finding a place to sleep that night. We were able to go in and see her throughout the night but it wasn't until morning that she opened her eyes.

She could hardly move and was in excruciating pain. As a man, it was extremely difficult to watch her suffer like that and not be able to do something about it. But as a father, it was Heaven just to see her alive. Alive. We could get through the pain and suffering, I was just happy that death was off of the table.

We would spend over two weeks at Children's Hospital watching our baby get better. Family and friends came from all around the area to check on Deja and us. The nurses became like family as well. We were there so long that we knew their shifts by heart. One of them even brought us dinner one night. The natural explorer in me had me navigating all of the hallways and back rooms of the hospital and I came to know the place like the back of my hand. I knew all of the shortcuts and hallways that traversed the facility like a country boy would know the woods behind his house.

Nighttime was the hardest for Deja. Nights always are. Even for me. *Even now.* Her aches seemed to worsen at night every night. She had this chart filled with smiley faces. The chart ranged from one to ten and as the numbers got bigger the faces gradually changed to sad faces. The doctor told us that a pancreas injury is one of the most painful injuries that a person can endure. It took over a week before Deja was able to point her tiny finger at anything under an eight. And even then I'd bet she was just being brave.

After the first week we really started noticing a change for the better. We caught the American Idol bug during our stay at the hospital and it seemed that the more Rubin sang the healthier Deja got. Before we knew it Deja was out of the bed and dragging her IV bag and pole up and down the hallway. So many people saw her naked butt hanging out of the hospital gown that I had to sneak some underwear on her. Turns out, she was going to be fine. Scarred up like her Daddy but fine. Thank you God and Children's Hospital.

I don't know if it is the fact that she is my first child that created the bond between us or if it is something else but Deja is a *Daddy's Girl* through and through. I worry sometimes that she might be trying too hard to make me happy. She has been like that all of her life and I have actually sat her down and talked to her about it. *"Daddy wants you to be happy. Don't do this for me. This is about you."*

I buy Deja and Desiree Redskin jerseys at the start of every football season. I have a little ritual that I follow each year. I buy Deja the jersey of the player that I want to see gone. Well, she wore her Redskins jersey to school the day after we lost to the Cowboys. Wow.

And it wasn't just any jersey either. It was big old number 8. Mark Brunell. *Remember my ritual?* She wore the jersey right after he blew one for us. I bet she still remembers that day. She said, *"Daddy, everyone kept asking me why I wore my Redskin jersey today. Did the Redskins lose?"* You see she didn't wear it because she watched the game, knew any better, understood the sport or how much Cowboys fan's suck. She wore it because it was clean and most importantly; she knew that her father loved to see her in it. I am sorry that my baby had to suffer because of a Redskins loss, believe me I know first hand the frustration that a happy Cowboy fan can cause. But on the bright side it is just one more thing that my baby and I have in common now.

Today Deja is ten, healthy and a budding softball star. She plays third base better than I could on my best day. She scoops up ground balls with a grace and grown up coordination that amazes me. And when she rockets the ball to first base, I am almost blown away sometimes. I hope she sticks with it. I think, as she gets older and better, softball could open some doors for her. But I try not to force anything. I try. Sometimes it is just so hard to control my excitement and pride.

I watched my baby hit a homerun today. She walked up to the plate with the confidence of *Casey at Bat*. After a few pitches, just like Casey, she was down to her last strike. Then all of the sudden, under the blazing July sun. Deja, mighty Deja, swung and whacked a homerun. She cracked the ball like Casey was supposed to. She hit the ball with such force and commitment that it sailed all the way to the outfield. The crowd went wild. My chest tightened as I stood there at the fence watching my baby round the bases. She crossed home plate standing up and humbly headed back to the dugout filled with bouncing and screaming teammates. What a sight to see. It was one of those forever moments for me. She handled the moment so quietly.

There was barely a smile on her face. But it was what she did next that touched me to my core and made me feel like I might be getting the hang of this *"Father Thang."*

I was still jumping up and down like a madman as Deja quickly weaved her way through the dugout filled with all of her screaming teammates and coaches, high-fiving each of them as she went by and came straight for me with her arms outstretched. Me. She came for me and hugged me tight. I felt like she was saying, *"That was for you, Daddy."* I am so thankful that I have children that make me proud. I am so happy that my children give me the opportunity to experience these feelings of pride and just plain old love. It is a beautiful thing.

I could've done that for my father. I could've made him proud. I know I could've.

I have played more than my share of innings of softball in my time but my tenure was short-lived. And that is because softballs are too hard and small. Why do they call them softballs anyway? Back in the pen I was on the Deep Meadow Correctional Center 5-A side champion softball team. I played left field and according to our coach, I didn't play it right. During our first game I ran up on a ground ball. As soon as I put my glove down the ball bounced off of a lump of grass and popped me right in the mouth. I thought it knocked my teeth out. I slammed my glove to the ground like a big baby, grabbed my mouth and stormed off the field with my lips throbbing. Instead of being a complete sissy and leaving the team, I decided to be the designated hitter and found that position a lot easier on my face.

Basketball is my game. It has always been. And I know that my father would have had many proud moments watching me on the court as I grew up. He would've been able to get up many times in the stands and yell proudly, *"That's my boy."* And now that I personally know the great delight that comes from watching your child succeed in something, I am that much more bewildered at how my father could choose to miss out on all the chances he would've had with me.

Deja's hospital experience was tough on all of us and it was there I first realized that I am a 90-pound weakling when it comes to my children. But the whole hospital thing also made our love stronger. We tell each other I love you every time we say good-bye. And we mean it. Hopefully the scary times are all behind us and all I have to worry about are sprained ankles and another broken bone or two. But I know better. It is a dangerous world and even more dangerous times that my babies are growing up in. And plus boys haven't even showed up to the party yet. Next to death, they are a father's worst nightmare. *Can you feel me shaking in my boots?*

4

"Dad, you're the Easter Bunny aren't you?"
-Desiree Corryn White

The only thing I hate more than a cell phone is a hospital. Our kids kept us there. When Desiree was six, we noticed that her voice was really deep. She sounded husky like Rita Cosby from MSNBC. We looked in her mouth and found that her tonsils were really swollen. We made an appointment with the doctor and found that she had to have her tonsils and adenoids removed. The procedure was to be performed out near Rockville, MD. A tonsillectomy is not a medical procedure that I think instills fear into most parents. I know I wasn't worried in the least. Before Desiree, if I heard tonsillectomy I thought of Cindy from the Brady Bunch and ice cream. Not anymore. That is because after the removal of her tonsils and adenoids, Desiree was not breathing correctly. It sounded like something was obstructed. Once again we had to stand there and face faces of confusion. The doctors at the surgical center were very concerned about Desiree and her breathing but were unable to do anything about it. So once again I was set off to follow another ambulance with my baby strapped inside. Children's Hospital here we come, again. I feel like I know that place better than Grandma's house up the country. We walked in to familiar faces and places. I even talked to the little light-skinned boy that the D.C. Sniper shot. T-Mac's little friend. Children's Hospital saved his life too.

Turns out that Desiree had nodules on her vocal cords and had to have them cut out.

Desiree never sounded *"right"* when she slept. In fact, there were several times that I woke her up out of a dead sleep because she didn't sound like she was breathing. Well, it turns out that when Desiree was put under anesthesia, there was a greater chance that she might not have come out of it. Considering how the nodules affected her breathing she could've suffocated. So, once again we found out that one of our children is lucky to be alive.

"That girl is Marcus with a ponytail." I hear all the time how much Desiree and I look alike. I saw the resemblance once in the bathroom mirror but never saw it again. No way could I possibly be that cute. She knows the words to every country music song that comes on the radio and loves animals. For some reason love doesn't seem to accurately describe the feeling that she has towards animals. One time I watched her chase down a toad at Kings Dominion, pick it up and put it in the grass so no one would step on it. That is an animal lover if I ever saw one. In her nine years she has given her love to at least 4 water turtles, 3 land dwelling tortoises from all over the world (Africa, Greece and Russia) 4 to 6 frogs, 2 dogs, a couple of parakeets and she is presently angling for a ferret and a pony. She even wants to write a book. Is that a little girl looking up to her Daddy or what? She asked me to read part of her book she was working on and I heard myself in her writing. It freaked me out.

"My Dad is the Redskins biggest fan. Sometimes when the Redskins play we go to my uncle's house. All the little kids play tag or something else and all of the grown-ups scream at the television. On my Dad's side of the family when the Redskins play it is like a holiday. It's like Christmas but you don't get presents. Instead you get your hair done. And trust me you do not want to get your hair done by Aunt Phyllis. It feels like she is heavy handed..."

I can't speak for everyone but not having a father always made me want to be a great one. I always knew that when I got my chance to be one I was going to do it right. I planned to be a Super Dad and do everything to make my children love me completely. But what does doing it right really entail? I always thought that Ward Cleaver had it right. But that was when I was a kid and was clueless as to what being a good father involved. I am a lot more tuned in now but I still don't have it down to a science. Does anyone??

Deja found a picture the other day. She looked up at me and said, *"Daddy, what position did you play on your team?"*

I said, *"What are you talking about?"*

She said, *"You are the only one with a red shirt on. Does that mean you were the captain?"*

I was dumbfounded for a second. *"Dej, what in the world are you talking about?"*

She handed me the picture and said, *"Daddy in this picture you are in front of the team and you are the only one dressed differently."*

At the time I was over 40,000 words into this book and believe it or not I couldn't find a single thing to say. The picture that she handed me was one of my old prison mob shots. The reason I was in front and dressed differently was because I was about to go home.

I thought to myself as I stood there looking at the mugged up faces of Petey, Super Dave and Shaji, *"How am I going to get out of this one?"*

It is amazing how fast your mind can work when you have a child staring up at you with eyes and ears demanding answers.

"Oh. You mean that picture? That is a picture of Daddy and some of the guys he used to work with when he was younger."

I was at the *"work"* camp when the photo was snapped, so it wasn't a lie. I did it the *"sneaky"* way because I believe that my kids are too young to have the *"Daddy went to prison"* talk. I just tell them that I was bad when I was younger. I feel that is all they need to know and I love it that they are shocked that I could ever be bad. It tells me a little bit about how they see me.

I chose to not be my girls' buddy. I'm the so-called disciplinarian. I give the orders and directions. But don't get me wrong though, I am still putty in their hands. I used to give ass whippings but it got to a point where they had to fight to hold in their laughter when I tried. Then eventually, thanks to my little comedian Miss Desiree, it got to a point where I had to hold in my own laughter when I tried. So I gave that nonsense up. I have to admit that sometimes I might be a bit hard on them but it is only because I know what is lurking out there in the world for them. I'm talking about the monsters. It is my job to protect my babies from them. I'm sure there are those that might have once thought of me as a monster. But the people that I consider to be the real monsters are rapists and pedophiles. I've lived with them. I've eaten breakfast, lunch and dinner with them and all the time I was sickened by them. And if that isn't enough, I have seen enough *"To Catch a Predator"* episodes and sex offender websites to know that there is a disgustingly ugly element sifting among our children. Therefore, if I have to be a little strict in order to improve their odds at having a happy and safe childhood, then so be it. As long as they love me at the end of the day then it is what it is.

And in case you were wondering, my children love me like birthday parties and ice cream cones. It is a fact that I am very proud of. It is also a fact that the love of your children is not a given. I don't love my father. Proof enough? Sure, just by being around, your children are going to love you as their father. But my girls *really* love me. When my children see me I get hugs and kisses, instead of groans and secret wishes that Daddy had to work late tonight. And that didn't just happen. I had to earn their love and it took work. If you ask them about their father, they will both straighten their face and say with the seriousness of a fire and brimstone preacher, *"My Daddy don't play."* But they are also the only ones I let see me act silly or hear me sing. They are not afraid of me and that is very important. I remember once we were over at my cousin's house. It was a nice house and was his first. I could tell he was very proud of it, as he should have been. He had one of those back in the day kind of living rooms. You know what I am talking about, the kind that kids were not allowed to be in. Looking back on it, I'm surprised he didn't have that thick clear plastic covering all of his furniture. His carpet was immaculate. It looked like no one had ever set a foot on it and I am sure that neither of his two kids would ever dare drink a cup of orange soda while standing on or anywhere within spilling distance of it. Notice that I said his kids. My kids, on the other hand, spill stuff. From baby bottles and sippie cups all the way to right now, my kids have left a Kool-Aid trail of red carpet stains that could have led Hansel and Gretel straight to the house in minutes. I remember when I was a kid, so some stuff I just don't take too seriously. Kids are going to make messes. That is what they do. But unfortunately everyone doesn't think like me. So when my cousin's little girl came running into the kitchen where the grown-ups were talking and said, *"Daddy, that girl spilled soda on the carpet."* I hoped there were not going to be any fireworks.

We walked into the living room and the kids were all huddled together staring at the Sunkist soda stain on the carpet like it was a dead bird. I remember their faces like it was yesterday. His kid's faces said, *"Oh my God. I can't believe she actually spilled soda on my Daddy's carpet. Someone is in big trouble and I am glad it isn't me."* My kid's facial expressions simply said, *"Oops."* But that is the point that I am trying to make. His kids were scared of him. I know they loved him but they were afraid of him, which is one thing I never want to happen to me.

I want my kids to grow old and look back on a happy childhood. A childhood filled with funny memories and instances that will forever bring a smile to their faces. I want them to remember good times. Like the time they caught me buying Easter baskets and candy at Giant. I want them to never forget the bedtime story that I used to tell them when they were four and five. The one where their Uncle Dre jumped out of the woods at the end of the story and yelled Booga! Booga! Boo! They loved that story so much they still ask me to tell it to them today. I just want them to know that I am so thankful for the joy that they have brought into my life. Without it, I just don't know.

I want them to know that it was as much a pleasure for me to evenly and neatly stack the presents around the Christmas tree, as I am sure it was for them ripping them open.

There were actually times on Christmas Eve that I could not sleep because of the anticipation of the kids waking up the next morning to a tree full of presents. Just like when I was a kid, every Christmas morning I am the first one up. I guess some things never change. But now I am up early for a different reason. Gone are the days of me running down the steps, anxious and siced to see how many Star Wars action figures I got from Santa Claus. Now I get to see the other side. Now I get to stand in my mother's shoes and watch pure joy. Now, because of Deja and Desiree, I know what she must have felt. The anticipation of seeing your child uncontrollably happy is a beautiful thing. In fact, the anxiety that I feel every Christmas Eve ranks up there with the night before I got out of prison.

In a single instant gone are all the labors and stress, caused by dealing with Scrooges, Grinches and the otherwise spiritless. My pocket drain and left foot pain caused from running store to store in the pouring rain all vanish the instant the kids wake up. The long lines in crowded stores and threats of never going to Wal-Mart no more all disappear the instant I hear my babies stirring in bed.

I make sure the kids always have a pretty tree. Christmas trees are important to me and have been ever since back in the day when ours used to sit in the corner of Grandma's living room. Ours was always filled with big, hot, multi-colored light bulbs and dozens of kid-made ornaments topped off with so much tinsel that the vacuum wouldn't pick it all up for years. When I look in the photo albums at our Christmas trees from yesteryear, sometimes I have to remind myself that there is actually a tree under all of the garland. From the looks of things Grandma just let us run wild with the decorations. And because of her attitude, which was kid first and carefree, nowadays I very anally decorate our Christmas tree. I make sure it is the perfect shape, height and I am very reserved when hanging bulbs and stringing lights. But most importantly, I make sure that underneath it is filled with as much of what the kids want as I can afford without landing myself in rent court. I remember my years of gazing at that big thick Sears Wish Book wishing I could get everything that I circled. My mother did the best she could and I remember how happy I felt seeing all of those presents on Christmas morning. So now, each year, PSP's, PS2's, camouflaged pants and rolling tennis shoes are all neatly wrapped and stacked under the tree. So many presents some years that they seem to flow out into the living room floor.

According to the rules of Miss Desiree, there must be two piles. And each pile must contain the same number of presents for each one of them or there is going to be a problem. One year Deja was still opening presents after Desiree finished and big time drama ensued. I still believe that Desiree just rushed through her presents faster than Deja but ever since then, after wrapping and tagging the presents, we do the count. It is a must and worth the time, believe me.

They always come out the same way on Christmas morning. They both act like they are not the least bit impressed by the tree full of presents and are too sleepy to open them up. As if they would rather go back to sleep for a couple of hours and then open up their gifts later. Yeah right. That little act lasts for only a minute or two because the next thing I know my living room looks like a back office on a late night at Enron. Shreds of paper everywhere. Desiree, a kid through and through, always goes for the hard presents first and leaves the soft ones for last. She figures that the soft presents are clothes and who needs those? That's my baby.

I did Christmas '06 myself. I had the tree. I had the presents. I had the turkey. And most importantly, I had the kids. Even though Chrisi and I had been apart for a few years we still all did Christmas together. 2006 was the first year we were not all together and I remember feeling a little sad about the realizations that I had that morning. The first realization being that Christmas was not going to be the same anymore and the next that I am not going to have a normal family in the traditional sense of the word. The kids live with her and I moved to the city but Christmas Eve and morning we were always together.

I love Christmas. It has always been my favorite holiday. As time has passed the importance of Christmas has evolved for me. As a child, it was about the toys. As an adolescent it was about my family. And now as a man it is about my girls.

My children never got to experience one of our full-blown Christmas' up at Grandma's house. I think Deja was just a baby the last time and I know Desiree wasn't even born yet. In 2006 I wanted my little one bedroom apartment in the hood to feel like Grandma's house up the country. I wanted Grandma and Ma to look down on me and feel proud.

The kids were as happy as could be that morning. The house was clean. The tree was shimmering perfectly and, with all the presents neatly stacked underneath, it made my living room looked like it should have been on a Christmas card somewhere. Everything was working out fine. All that was left was the food. The house needed to smell like turkey, only then would it really feel like Christmas. I am a very picky eater and because of that my cooking skills are limited pretty much to scrambled eggs and Steak-umms. My Christmas menu was filled with several items that I don't personally eat so I had to reach out to some of my work mamas for recipes and tips. I felt pretty good about my turkey plans. It was the macaroni and cheese that was really stressing me. And other than my sister Joan's version, corn pudding died with Grandma and Ma. But I was up for the challenge.

No one from the family called with any plans to get together so I wasn't expecting any one other than Chrisi and the kids for dinner. Fortunately, I am a White and the last thing we run out of at Christmas is food. I said fortunately because not long after noon I started getting calls. It seems that word spread around the family that I was cooking and evidently the sight of me in the kitchen was a must see. That turned my quaint and quiet Christmas with the kids into a loud and crowded Christmas with my family. And it was perfect. I mean there was a minor mishap or two like my kitchen getting smoked out from the corn pudding that I tipped over in the bottom of the oven or the macaroni and cheese being a little too loose but all in all it was a good day, a really good day. My sisters came over with their kids and my Aunt Phyl came by with her two kids, my Uncle Howard showed up feeling pretty good and before I knew it, my apartment far exceeded its capacity. We all laughed, talked, ate and watched the kids open up more presents. What was left of the corn pudding was the hit of the day and my greens and cabbage turned out to be really good too. But most importantly, the turkey was the bomb and I had enough of it left over for a week of late night sandwiches.

I have a photo from that day. It is one of Deja and Desiree hugging each other in front of the Christmas tree. It is funny to me because I haven't seen the two of them hug since that day. The picture is a reminder to me of one of the many good moments that my children and I have had together. But our life hasn't always been as pretty as the picture of the two of them sitting cross-legged in front of a lit up Christmas tree with the dog and turtles. There have been hard times too and I am not talking about a long night in a dark hospital room. I'm talking about things like separation and Mommy's new boyfriends.

5

"I claim not to have controlled events but confess plainly that events have controlled me."

-Abraham Lincoln

My mother's little brother John has been the favorite uncle for over two generations of White children. That isn't to say that we didn't love our Uncle's Terry and Howard but John just always had a way with children and still does today. He somehow has the ability to transform himself into a Newport smoking, Budweiser drinking, shit talking, gray-haired child and I haven't seen a kid yet that didn't love him.

John got married young. I think he was like twenty-one or twenty-two. His new wife was named Toni. She was tall, light skinned and very pretty. I was the ring bearer in their wedding and fortunately I was too young to realize that the orange tuxedoes with ruffled peach colored shirts and bowties would have landed us on top of Huggy Low Down's list of Bamas of the Week. I remember after the wedding, when it was time for pictures to be taken, no one knew where I was. My Aunt Phyl eventually found me hanging up side down in one of the church trees with my cousin Barry. Considering that I was dressed like a damn fruit I'm wondering why the trees weren't the first place they looked.

The night before the wedding I stayed the night at my Uncle Howard's house with my three uncles. When I flash back to that night, I always see the three of them sitting around a kitchen table. I don't know if that is just my mind working on its own or if that is actually where they were before I fell asleep. I don't really remember anything that they did that night, I don't think they snuck in a hooker after I went to bed but knowing the three of them I am sure there was a lot of noise and plenty of empty Budweiser cans in the trash can by night's end.

The next morning we woke up late. I remember all of us frantically rushing around the house trying to get ready. That's when it happened. When I pulled my fruit-colored pants up, I ripped the hem in one of my pant legs. I heard the rip but didn't see exactly what ripped. It wasn't until my Uncle Howard walked up and said, *"Boy? What the hell you do to your pants?"* that I realized I had messed up. We had to rush to the tuxedo rental place to get it fixed and then head to the church. I remember walking into the tuxedo shop with one pants leg longer than the other and the guy that had just fitted me the day before put both his hands up to his cheeks in disbelief like McCauley Caulkin and was like, *"Oh my."* It took him about fifteen minutes to get my pants back in order and the clock was still ticking. We were going to be late. Looking back on it that should have been a sign for us to grab another case of beer and head back to Howard's house and party like rock stars. But obviously we didn't and the wedding went off as planned. I remember it being a happy and *"colorful"* day.

Not long after the wedding John and Toni had a baby boy, John J.W. White. He grew to be a cute little good-haired boy that looked just like a light skinned version of his father. John adored his son. Adored. John White loves everybody's kids so you can imagine how much he would love his own.

Eventually, for one reason or probably many, John and Toni split up. John was driving a truck back then and spent a lot of time away from home. That didn't help things and caused lots of problems. On top of that he was suffering from a chemical imbalance. The imbalance caused John to overreact to and angrily address minor issues. That caused more problems. Toni would leave. Then she would come back. Then she would leave again only to return. Finally, trying to solve too many problems became an unsolvable problem, so she packed her bags, took J.W. with her and left for good, leaving John wandering in a maze of frustration. I was young but I remember that John was messed up for a while after that.

I was around nine or ten years old on the evening that I overheard my Uncle John on the phone with his son. It was over twenty-five years ago and I remember it as clear as the rain from yesterday. It was around 5'oclock on a Sunday evening and there was a football game on the television when the phone rang. I didn't mean to listen to the conversation but John was standing so close to me that I couldn't help but hear. His voice was cheery and his tone was happy. From the smile on his face I could tell he was talking to his son. Obviously I couldn't see what happened next but from John's reaction I could very plainly, even at my age, tell what happened. During the call J.W. must have called his mother's new boyfriend Daddy. I listened as John tried to explain to his young son that the other nigga was not his Daddy. He questioned him and explained over and over again and I could tell it was eating him up. Finally, J.W. must have replied, *"You are Daddy too."*

What happened next scarred and scared me.

In a split second my Uncle John's face morphed from a father smiling and happy to hear from his son into that of a monster. The Incredible Hulk and Mike Tyson come to mind as I sit here. I watched the pain spread out across his face and down his neck like thin ice cracking after it had been stepped on. His muscles were flexed and his veins stood so tall that even a blind dope fiend couldn't miss them. His back hunched over, he gripped the arm of the sofa and looked almost weak in the knees. But weak was just the outward appearance. Weak is just what his knees looked like. Inside was where the rage, violence and pain were invisibly stretching his heartstrings to the floor like the longbows of a million Persian warriors. And when the arrows were loosed, *they blocked out the sun.*

John hung up the phone and proceeded to tear up Grandma's house. He flipped chairs and tables. He knocked pictures off the wall and then he looked me dead in my face with tears streaming down his cheeks and screamed in disbelief, *"Daddy too? You are Daddy too? I can't believe that shit Marc!! I can't believe it!!"*

It was one of the most frightening experiences of my life. I didn't move a muscle and sat as still as a stone in that maelstrom of fury and wrath. I sat still even as I felt the sting of his hot breath piercing the pores of my face. At that point in my life I had never seen such an explosive combination of hurt and anger. It was a terrifying experience to witness someone that up to that point had always been smiling and happy, change into a house wrecking, fitful and fearsome human being. At nine or ten years old I didn't fully understand how the love of your children could instantly turn into a murderous rage. But at thirty-five I understand it well.

Inside I knew that eventually Chrisi was going to find a new guy and bring him around my kids. I not only knew that but I also knew what the nigga was gonna look like. A tall dark skinned Jamaican with long dreads. I knew all of that with absolute certainty but I forced myself to not believe it, if that makes any sense.

I remember the day I found out how smart I was. Deja had softball practice so Chrisi and the kids met me at the metro station and we all rode to practice together. I remember thinking when I first sat in the car that something smelled funny. Thanks to the kids, Chrisi's cars were always a mess. So because of that I was used to getting in and smelling French fries, fried chicken or some other food item that the kids decided to leave in the floor of the car instead of putting in the trash. But this smell was different. It didn't smell like candy, kids or potato chips. This smelled like a nigga. Like a nigga's feet. And if he left a dirty smell in a dirty car then, to me, he was a dirty nigga.

Now before you start with your, *"Marc, you didn't want her so she had the right to find someone else."* comments. Let me tell you this. This was not about Chrisi. Getting your groove back is one thing. But getting your groove back when you have two young daughters in the house is a horse of a different color. Even Stella knew that much. You don't meet a nigga in some sweaty ass club and then have him waking up around your daughters a week or two later. You get the nigga in and out before the kids wake up. Especially when the kid's father is still in the picture. I just felt it was disrespectful. To me and to the kids.

The whole time Deja was practicing, Chrisi's cell phone was blowing up. It struck me as odd but I went on ignoring it. She handles a lot of issues at her job and I figured that maybe something was going on at work that needed her input. But when we were in the car, headed back to drop me off, her phone continued to ring constantly but she wouldn't answer it. I asked, *"Why don't you answer your phone?"* She said, *"I don't want to disrespect you."* I was taken aback and was like, *"Who is it? Your boyfriend?"* She didn't say anything. I could tell she was nervous. Then finally she said, *"Yeah."* I turned my head in disgust and looked in the backseat. The kids looked terrified. I asked her, *"The kids met him?"* She hesitated for what felt like an eternity and then she said, *"Yeah."* I looked in the backseat again and the kids were crying.

All I could think about was, *"You are Daddy too."*

I was intentionally kept in the dark and was hurt to my core. Not so much by Chrisi, she hurt my ego a little but the kids knowing about this nigga and the fact that they were instructed to keep it from their father crushed me. Why teach your *daughters* to keep secrets from their father? What sense does that make? No one in Deja and Desiree's life knows better how crazy this world can be than me. And when they get older and their own worlds get crazy, I want them to know they have someone well versed in world craziness on their side. Why would you take that from them? Why take that from me? I want my kids to glide over all the holes I fell in and they can't do that with secrets.

As we drove down the GW Parkway headed to the city I stared straight ahead through the dirty windshield. For a split second I thought about grabbing the wheel and sending all four of us careening into the Potomac. That was the *"Daddy too"* pain starting to take affect. But I kept my roaring inside. When I'm angry my legs jump. My right leg was pounding the floor like a jackhammer and at times seemed like it would crash through the metal to the pavement below. I kept my tears invisible and just let them coat the back of my throat. I felt like I couldn't get home fast enough. My right hand gripped the interior door handle tight like my Uncle John gripped the arm of Grandma's living room sofa, all the time I was wishing I could wrap it around Chrisi's neck. When we got to my house not only did I get out of the car quickly and without any kisses goodbye, I also got out of the car wanting to kill somebody.

When I came inside, I didn't tear my house up. I didn't cry. I didn't kick the dog or rip paintings off the wall. Instead, I unplugged the phone, rolled up a Backwood, sat in the dark and contemplated murder.

6

"Becoming a father is easy enough but being one can be very rough"
-Wilhelm Busch

People say that the apple doesn't fall far from the tree. In the case of my father and me I like to think that the apple not only fell far from the tree but it also rolled down a hill, off a cliff and landed on a banana boat. That nigga didn't teach me anything and I suffered because of it. Check that. I am suffering because of it.

Instead of a father, it was prison that helped me to become a man. It taught me to be tougher. It taught me to be independent. Problem is prison didn't teach me how to be a *"good man."* And it definitely didn't prepare me for adult relationships. I learned later in life that those years in the pen would cost me more than just some separation and time. When I should have been dating and learning how to treat women I was playing pool and basketball with felons. I was ignorant of a woman's needs. I had a teenager's brain in a grown man's body. When I came home, others my age were settling down and doing right. I just wanted to run. And I ran like Carl Lewis used to. Eventually, I couldn't run the race as fast as before and the tortoise caught up to me and beat my ass like I spray-painted graffiti on his shell. It cost me everything. And by everything I mean an everyday relationship with my children. Does anything else really matter?

I met my kid's mother, Chrisi, through her brother Greg. Greg and I were introduced by the Virginia Department of Corrections. Greg is what I call a *"cool white boy."* The type that is more at home on a basketball court full of brothers or in a smoked out living room, playing Madden in the hood than... *thinking... still thinking*, ok, wherever it is the white boys hang out; Old Navy, maybe??

Chrisi and I hit it off from the jump. Which is odd considering that we are both Libras. (I know now to ask the sign. It matters, I'm serious.) Even thought we talked on the phone for hours and saw each other every day before and after work, I didn't see Chrisi and get the instant vibe that she and I were meant to be together. I didn't see her and automatically think that she was *"The One."* Remember I still had my track shoes on. I wanted to get on with my life, so step one as far as I was concerned was getting out of my Aunt Phyllis' house.

Considering how I feel about Chrisi at times, it is hard saying this. Really hard. But I do have to give her some credit for helping me become who I am. She moved me into her house and basically took care of me like I was her child for the first few months when I came home. She bought me clothes. Polo shirts and they are not cheap. She gave me lunch money and made sure I got to computer class on time. She was down for me and that is part of the reason why I try to do right by her now even though a lot of the time I am sickened by her decisions.

I hate to reiterate this fact but I need to make it clear that I was young in age and even younger in thinking when I first came home from prison. That being said, there were so many things that Chrisi wanted out of a relationship that were miles away from my thinking. I wanted to party, hang out at the basketball court and try to make up for lost time. Chrisi wanted to be a family. I just wasn't ready. I was thinking like a teenager, so marriage and forever never crossed my mind. Even after the kids came I still didn't feel like I was in the right place. Physically or mentally.

One time I gave Chrisi a hint about one of her Christmas presents. Like an idiot I told her that her present was seven letters and it started with a *"D."* When Christmas came around and there were **D R Y**

W A L L plans for a remodeled kitchen that I was planning for her under the tree instead of a **D I A M O N D** ring, let's just say it was the beginning of the end.

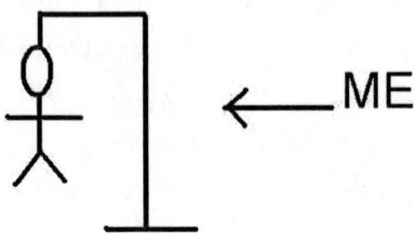

But we had kids and as far as I thought, I had to be there. Leaving the house meant leaving the kids and I couldn't do that. I had to break the cycle. I didn't want to be like my father in any way so I stayed and was miserable. And since misery loves company, I decided to bring Chrisi along for the ride. The kids too.

It was a messy time and I am glad it is over. In my dreams I wish I could just add Chrisi to my list of failed relationships and move on. I would like nothing more than to just have her as a memory but her being the mother of my children makes that impossible.

Even though this is Chapter 6, it is really the last chapter written. The rest of my book has been finished for weeks. I was so worried about how I was going to write this chapter and what I was going to write in it that I just blocked it from my mind until I had no choice but to sit here and write it. I just jumped right from Chapter 5 to Chapter 7 and kept on writing. And even as I was breezing through Chapters 7 through 24 I knew all the time that Chapter 6 was still sitting back there in the room waiting for me to come in and face it.

From the very beginning I had planned for Chapter 6 to be my longest and most in depth chapter detailing as much as I could remember about my relationship with Chrisi. I was going to completely expose myself. But then I thought about it and realized that doing that would not be right.

So I am choosing to not go into detail about all the things that went wrong with my relationship with Chrisi. That is a book that she is going to have to write. And if she chooses to do so, she has my blessing. I am making the decision to be vague because even though this is my book, my life and actions still affected others and to put their business in the street is not the right move and is not what I am about. Plus, with me, it is either all or nothing. I can't do things half way. There was no way that I could go all out with this chapter and not hurt someone that doesn't deserve it or might be trying to heal and get on with their life. I will just say that in the end Chrisi and I were both guilty of acts that were deemed unforgivable and our relationship as we knew it, was kaput. Period.

It is difficult now having to share the kids and this new twist in my relationship with Chrisi still feels weird to me. But I know our separation is for the best and lately there have even been times that we actually seem to like each other again. *There is a God.*

7

> *"You are wrong Marcus, because it says right here in the Bible that..."*
> *-Too many people to count.*

For someone that has spent as many hours in church as I have, you would think that I would be a religious person. I am not. And it may come as a shock to some when I say that I don't believe in God in the traditional sense that I was raised to believe in Him. Unlike a lot of people, I'm not afraid to say that I don't know what, who or where God is. I am smart and *"touched"* enough to know that there is someone or something somewhere that protects us but am not so well versed in the subject matter that I can say for fact anything else.

I think my views on religion have come from confusion. I have intersected with too many false prophets and they have allowed me to see clearly their artificial ways. The two-faces and lies of many so-called men of God made me ill and eventually planted the seeds of doubt. Not doubt of whether or not there is a God. Believe me I am straight with that. My misgivings lie with man. In my time I thought that because you put on a robe, hung a cross around your neck and stood up in front of the church every Sunday, you were *"a man of God."* Now I know that just isn't true in all cases. So many men and women today claim to be *"called"* to spread the word of God simply because they took a course and got some letters behind their name. For most of my life I was blinded by what I was told. For years I was allowed to be filled with life directing thoughts and ideas by people that I believed knew what they were talking about. The strict lessons that were pounded into me from childhood kept me from thinking. They kept me from asking, *"What does it really mean to be a man of God?"* I don't know yet but it has to be something more than just having the ability to perform Saturday afternoon wedding ceremonies and Sunday morning sermons.

Much more than a robe and cross and on another level a whole lot less than either of them, I simply believe that my God wants me to love my fellow man. I believe that my God doesn't want all of the credit and wants me to do for me. I believe that my God wants me to love my neighbor regardless of whether he has accepted a savior or not. I believe that my God loves the man that loves his fellow man. I believe that my God cares for the family that forgoes Sunday morning church service to service the hungry *so others might eat*. I believe that my God loves the foreign aid worker that gave up a modern and contemporary life in the States to travel deep into the jungles of Africa to spend her nights rocking AIDS infected babies to sleep. My God loves the homeless and the people that help them. Talk is cheap. My God loves the people that walk the walk. I feel that those are the *"religious"* ones in His eyes. I feel that the giving of yourself to help those in need is more important than pretending to give yourself to God.

I remember the day I walked to the front of the church where Reverend Smith was standing with his right hand of fellowship held high in the air asking the congregation, *"Is there one?"* Looking back on it I only went up front to join church because my cousins Barry, Tony and Kim had already done it. My decision wasn't something that I discussed with anyone. It wasn't something that I pondered during the weeks and days leading up to it. I just saw Terry Thompson stand up and walk down the aisle and I figured that no way was he gonna beat me too. So I got up and willingly agreed to give my 12-year-old life to Christ without paying any respect to the small print. But that was then. I'm grown now and I am more apt to question shit.

The only Kool-Aid I drink is the Kool-Aid I make and I like it with lots of sugar. Which means I am not so quick to follow suit and that

I like my Kool-Aid with lots of sugar.☺ I am spiritual, not religious and I feel that my relationship with God is as it should be. A personal one. The personal part is very important to me and because of that I normally keep my views to myself, especially since they have strayed away from the *"norm."* And since I have found my own way to God I have learned not to talk about Him or religion with people other than family. I do this because God and religion are both serious and touchy topics and can change a person's opinion of you faster than a prison sentence.

I don't claim to know everything about God and I wish so many others could be as honest about the unknown as I am. All I know is that He exists and that He loves me. That's it. And really, isn't that enough? So many are so blinded by faith and stuck waiting on miracles that they cannot see reality and end up waiting forever for their happiness instead of hunting for it.

Excuse me Reverend. Don't shoot. Because I didn't say nothing about your piccolo player and I also do not regard the Bible as being literally the word of God. To me the Bible is God's word as written by man. That is where it has lost me. From the beginning of time, man has proven to be fallible, deceitful and easily corrupted. My God has never spoken to me directly nor has He ever appeared to me in any type of mysterious form. There have been events and moments throughout my life that I believe were inspired or instrumented by a higher power and I always thank my God for them but honestly who really knows what inspired or instrumented them? No one. So when people say to me that God told them to do something or that God spoke to them, my first inclination is to tell them that they are full of shit. I have seen a miracle, a real one with my own eyes and if God has yet to find the time to talk to me and clue me in on what I saw then why would I believe that He would clarify His will to this preacher and that? I don't. If something happens in your life that makes you see things in a different light then say that. Tell me that seeing your friend in jail made you decide to live legally. Tell me that watching your mama die made you decide to be more concerned about your health. Say that and you will keep creditability with me. Say God spoke to you and *"told"* you to change and you lose me. I'm not even listening anymore. I'm wondering if the Skins are going to win that weekend, what the kids are doing or what I missed on The Sports Junkies that morning.

My take on God and religion has evolved from a massive theological lesson filled with pictures of a bearded white man dying on a cross to save my life and a thick black book full of words and names that I could never pronounce. Eventually, after many twists and turns, my views transformed into a very plain and simple idea. I believe that we all have something to accomplish while we are here. For some of us those goals are achieved quickly and our time here on Earth is brief. For instance, the birth of a premature infant with minutes to live could provide seconds of joy that turn out to be the glue that holds together its parents failing marriage. That's a short life with an intention and it happens everyday. For others it may take seventy and eighty years to finally complete our task. And that blind search for purpose will lead us through life. When our job is done, our time is up and off we go. Where? I don't know. I'm not sure if there is a Heaven but I like to think there is.

I also don't know if there is a hell either and I don't think people should use the unseen flames to scare sense into or the shit out of children. Check this out.

I was probably nine, ten or eleven years old *(Those ages all blend together.)* when our church invited a fire and brimstone preacher to come and speak. If you have never witnessed one, let me tell you, for me it was a terrifying experience. Especially since I was a kid. I sat in church on a weeknight and watched as this white man showed the congregation of our church a movie. The movie was about a family with two teenage sons. One son was basically a good child. He went to church with his mother. He said his prayers. He didn't drink, smoke or have sex. He did all the things that he thought God required. His older brother on the other hand was the exact opposite. While his mother and younger brother were in church, the older brother was at home downing cans of beer with his father, cussing and watching football games. The parents squabbled constantly over the two different roads their boys were taking. The mother prayed and prayed for a conversion in her oldest son but before her prayers could be answered, he was killed, without an ounce of repentance, on the track in a horrible car racing accident.

This is where my young mind was blown away.

The next thing I know I am sitting straight up and asshole tight in the Mount Olive Baptist Church of Rectortown watching the older brother literally burning in hell. I am talking about blood, flames, screams of agony and even a horned devil. At that time in my life, I hadn't even been introduced to Freddy Krueger, Jason Vorhees or Michael Myers yet. I'm serious when I say that the very first horror movie I ever watched in my life was seen at my church. How crazy is that? I couldn't wait for that movie to be over. Little did I know, the worst was yet to come. After the movie ended and the kids could breathe again, the white guy got up in the pulpit and proceeded to scream and holler about drinking and cussing and sex and how all of them were gonna send our black asses straight to hell. What did he know? I mean for real. What did he know for real? I'd bet my life that it wasn't anything factual. Am I supposed to believe that just because he had the title of preacher that he was doing God's will? Am I supposed to believe that God literally wanted the hell scared out of a church full of children? WTF?

The one thing that religions all have in common is that there is always a higher power. There is always someone or something to answer to when you mess up. It's like having to go to the Principal's Office when you are a third grader knowing the paddle with the holes in it is sitting in the corner. That is another reason I veered off the path. I can't allow myself to love a God that wants me to be afraid of him. I believe that my God wants love and appreciation, not fear. And as I sat there in church that night all I felt was fright. I remember when it was time to leave, getting up out of the pew and speeding out the church like on a Sunday afternoon when the Redskins game was already on.

There are many different religions. At times it seems like too many. Who is right? Is anyone? And if someone turns out to actually be right, what happens to the millions that are wrong? The white preacher from back in the day couldn't be right. His methods were just too ugly. I remember a time when I thought religion was just seeing your cousins and friends every Sunday. It was beautiful. Back in the days when my grandmother could walk to church, it was like family. It was pure. It was small and welcoming. I used to love going to church. I couldn't wait for it sometimes. Now it is something else. I think I have witnessed the diluting of God and religion. Something totally different. I am almost glad that my grandmother is not here to witness it. Although she would have been proud to see how good for the job Rocky has become and proudly surprised that little Verdice turned out to be a preacher, she would still have seen our sad state of affairs and said to me, *"Marc, we are living in the last days."* And I would have believed her. I do believe her. Now it seems like it is all about how many sinners your church can hold, who is wearing what or how many Benzes are in the parking lot. This tells me one thing. That religion has become corrupted by--guess who? Man. And for that reason I choose not to subscribe to it.

However, I do give respect to Jesus but not because of anything I ever heard in a church sermon. I give love and respect to Jesus because my grandmother did and I saw something save her life one night. Jesus was her savior so I'm giving him the credit.

I was sitting in the living room with my sisters and my mother watching television one evening and we all heard a really loud pop come from outside. I jumped up out of the floor and was the first one through the front door. I stopped in amazement on the porch because my grandmother was standing in the middle of the street seemingly frozen stiff.

"Look both ways before you cross the street." "Don't play too close to the road." Those were warnings that we all heard from the time we were old enough to play outside. The house we grew up in was situated fifteen yards back off the road and set on a straight stretch coming out of a blind curve. Crossing the street was always dangerous for us, even pulling out in cars and I know that living so close to it must have scared my mother to death.

Grandma used to work in Fairfax, Virginia. Actually, it was Falls Church to be more specific. She never learned to drive a car, so she depended on others to get around. So every morning she got up before the sun, had her coffee and then watched through the window for either Buck or Turner to pull up and drive her and a few other ladies to Fairfax to clean rich ladies' homes. For years I can remember her stirring around in the kitchen hours before the school bus arrived. I miss the smell of her coffee in the morning.

In the evening, Grandma would get dropped off right in front of the house, usually around 6:00 P.M. or so. Most times we would be in the yard playing and run up to greet her as she made her way up the steps after a long day and ride. But on the night I am about to talk about we were all in the house.

Every time I can ever remember seeing Grandma get out of the car after work she always exited from the passenger-side rear, walked around in front of the car, looked both ways and then crossed the street. Every time without fail she always got out of the car on the curbside and absolutely never did she get out directly into the street. For some reason on this night she exited the car from the driver-side rear and stepped right into the path of oncoming traffic. As soon as Grandma closed the door a carload of teenagers came flying around that blind curve I was talking about earlier. Grandma should have been dead. Her body should have been mangled and thrown halfway past Aunt Will's house. But she wasn't dead. Very much alive, she was standing there in the street like Lady Liberty with her bags still in hand and a blank look on her face.

By the time she made it up the steps and out of the street the kids were back and they pulled into our yard. It was four white teenagers. Two boys and two girls and they all looked to be about seventeen or eighteen. The two guys looked scared and both of the girls were crying uncontrollably. I bet the few seconds that passed with them being unsure about whether or not they ran down a little old lady were the things that movies are made of. We all stood in the yard wondering what had just happened. The kids were sure they hit "*something*." That is why they turned around. Ma, Jean, Joan and I definitely heard "*something*." That is why we went running outside. But everything was fine. Grandma wasn't injured. All the dogs were accounted for. No cars were damaged. What the hell happened?

I've told the story a few times but only to people that I know will not look at me like I'm crazy. I just wish I had been older when this all happened so I could have talked about it with Grandma. As hard as I try to remember, I can never recall us mentioning that evening to her nor her volunteering any personal thoughts on the event. The memory of that evening has been a constant in my thoughts ever since I saw it go down. To say that day has affected me would be an understatement to say the very least. It pains me when I think about not talking to her because I feel like I really missed out on something. Some form of higher learning. I'm sure she would have said that Jesus saved her. I just wish I had asked. I just wish I could have heard her tell me what she thought when she saw that car flying around the curve. Or what the wind felt like as it sped by. What did she see? Did she feel anything? There are so many questions that I foolishly let go to the grave with her. If only I had asked just one time, "*Grandma, what do you think happened that night in the street?*"

This is what I think.

We each have someone or something that looks out for us and makes sure we get our "*job*" done. You say angels I say watchers. Either way, those entities act as bodyguards shielding us from the everyday perils of life on this planet. Whatever was assigned the job of looking after my grandmother was obviously so used to her exiting the vehicle from the passenger-side rear that he decided he could squeeze in a quick coffee break at the same time she was about to climb out of the car. But when he finished his latte and got back to his desk, he saw the car full of kids screaming around the curve. He realized what was about to happen, checked his database and saw that it was not my grandmother's time. Therefore he was forced to act quickly. His only resort, according to the disaster recovery plan, was to break the emergency glass and George Bush the button, placing a shield around my grandmother at the last second, saving her life and exposing the existence of some strange shit to a yard full of people all wondering, *"What the hell just happened?"* I wonder if the *"Watcher"* got a write up or put on a performance improvement plan for his error.

I don't believe that Grandma was saved because she was a good God-fearing woman. I mean she was definitely a good God-fearing woman but I feel she was spared for another reason. Even I have been spared so I don't think being good or God-fearing is a mandatory qualification for an unexplainable life-saving event. Check this. I have been pulled over on the side of the road, surrounded by five white cops, with a pound of weed in the trunk of my car and walked away from the whole ordeal with just a ticket for falsified tags in my hand instead of my black ass in the can. I hopped the jersey wall and stood on the side of the highway and watched as the police had the car, with all of my smoke in the trunk, towed away to the impound lot. I stood there clouded in disbelief wondering, *"Damn, how did I make it out of this one?"* They had me dead to rights. All they had to do was pop the trunk and I would have been ghost like Casper's ass. Straight to jail nigga. Do not pass go. Do not collect $200. But for some strange reason they didn't. They tore the inside of the car up but never checked the trunk. Why? Isn't that police procedure and one of the first places you are supposed to check when you got a young black man in the crosshairs on the side of the road? Where the hell was the dog? Why the hell am I still here? Why didn't they check the damn trunk? I ask myself those questions all the time. Why did Grandma live? That's another question that occupies a lot of my brain time. I feel that she and I were both saved for the same reason. Neither of us had completed our task yet. Our family went through a lot after that night in the street. We needed Grandma. We needed her to get through my Uncle Terry's sickness and death. We needed her to get through my prison sentence. We needed her. That is why she wasn't snatched away from us that evening in the road. Because as bad as it got for us, it would have been a lot worse if she were not there to guide us through the black tunnels of turmoil that faced our family in the years to come. She is gone now, her task finally complete after seventy-one years. I'm still here grieving her passing at thirty-five so obviously my task is not.

8

"Terry knew he was going to die. So we didn't talk about living. We talked about dying."

-Reverend N.W. Smith, Mt. Olive Baptist Church

My daughter, Desiree, has had to spend her whole short life being told how much she resembles her father. I can relate with her because I have endured the same treatment and I hope she takes the observations as a compliment like I always do when it happens to me. I have been told, from my youth all the way up to now, that I look like my Uncle Terry and I love it. Kelvin Terry White. What a man he was. He was cool. I am talking about Fonzi kind of cool. He was sharp, stylish and always GQ smooth. I have pictures of him from back in the Cooley High days that could have been on an Ebony magazine cover. It is no wonder that he drove the ladies crazy.

Anything that was ever broken he could find a way to fix it. He was a whiz at repairing a variety of household breakables. I am talking about everything from sewing machines and clock radios to televisions and Hi-Fi stereos. You name it, we broke it and he would always fix it. As White children, it is mandatory that you always love your mama. I said always and Terry White was no exception. He used to come to Rectortown from Manassas on a Saturday morning and would not leave until everything Grandma needed fixed or moved or made was complete. Sometimes we would be asleep when he arrived at the house and then back asleep again before he left. Grandma was always like, *"Terry is coming, so he will take care of it. Terry is coming... Terry is coming...Terry is coming..."* She was so proud of him and his abilities. I think she felt like she did things right with him. That isn't to say that she messed up with John and Howard because that wasn't the case at all. And that is also not to say that Terry didn't mess up a time or three himself. I'm just saying that Grandma and Terry had a special connection. It was obvious. I think it was because of what happened to my little cousin Shawn.

I was fourteen years old when my Uncle Terry died. He was thirty-one. So young, I know. I told you in my first book that the good ones always seem to check out early in my family. *Hmm, I was wondering why I'm still here. Maybe that's why.* I have always felt like I was gonna die young. I don't know if that feeling is from just not wanting to get old or if it comes from something else. In the years since his death I have found several links between my Uncle Terry and myself. To me those links add further credence to my belief that I will not live long enough to have to worry about what Geritol tastes like. Below are a few of the consistencies that I have found.

Number one. He was a fixer of many things, especially electronics and if you needed someone to hook up something he was always your first call. I fix computers and believe me; I couldn't even begin to tell you how many people have a computer guy list with my name at the very top of it. Number two. Women loved him. He had photo albums filled with so many pictures of pretty girls that it would take me forever to read all the writing on the backs of them. It was funny because on the back of each picture were words expressing great affection. They all seemed to love his ass. I used to keep the photo albums stacked in my room like they were porno magazines and I even had favorites. Women happen to love me. It is hard saying that without feeling like an arrogant jerk but it is true. I am not nearly the chick magnet that my Uncle Terry was but I do see women checking me out all the time. Am I trippin'? Maybe a little but wait there is more. Three. My Uncle Terry fathered two daughters that loved him like freeze pops and Tootsie Rolls; Missy and Jennifer, one of which looks exactly like him. I happen to spend a lot of time cleaning up after two little girls myself and they love me to death. And guess what? One of them happens to look just like me. Four. I look like him. One time I stopped by to see his wife, Margie and after walking up the way to greet her, she said that for a second she thought I was my uncle coming down the sidewalk. *"Boy you look so much like Terry White that I thought he had come back to me."* That was his former wife telling me that but I have heard it from everyone. I don't know. It might be a little odd but I pay attention to stuff like that.

My Uncle John was the best ball player of my trio of uncles but my Uncle Terry was always the fastest. I remember at cookouts, John and Terry always arguing about who was the fastest. The next thing you know the whole family is all lined up in the yard watching John and Terry's backs as they both head fifty yards or so down to the Branch, talking trash to each other the whole way. *(There was a stream that ran perpendicular across the bottom of our property. We always called it The Branch. Don't ask me why because I don't know.)* When they would get to The Branch, they would turn around and wait for Phyl or Sherry to raise and drop their hands. Of course, there was always guaranteed to be a false start or two. It was so exciting to watch as the both of them came blazing up from the bottom of the field like two thoroughbreds. The muscles in their arms were taut and sun and sweat combined to make their skin sparkle like one of Puff Daddy's Rolexes. With their legs pumping like pistons and their faces staring angrily straight ahead, they would streak right past all of us and sometimes get nearly to the house before they could slow down. Sometimes they would come charging through within inches of us and I could feel the wind as they would rush past and the ground trembling under my feet. At some point towards the end of race, Terry would always pull ahead and glance over to John with a smile as they were running, I guess as a way to let John know that he was beat. The next part was always my favorite. That is when we would all sit around on picnic tables eating and listening to the two of them both, very animatedly, claim victory. John would say, *"Terry knows he cheated. He jumped the start!"* Terry would say, *"Shit, the nigga was bumping me the whole way up!"* Both would make compelling and hilarious arguments which usually led to another race. Damn, I loved being a kid.

I remember the last race I saw John and Terry run. Terry lost. I was mad at John afterwards for calling him out because he knew Terry was sick. By then, we all did. But I don't have a brother so I don't know firsthand the rivalry that can exist between two of them. John had been trying for years to beat Terry so I guess he was so caught up in the moment that he didn't see a sick and weakened Terry White that he was challenging to a race. He just saw Terry White, his brother that he almost always challenged to a race. Plus at that time none of us knew just how sick Terry really was. So I sat there and watched as one of my heroes got smoked on the same field where just a year ago he was doing all the smoking. When the race was over, instead of screams of delight there were only moments of fright because Terry was doubled over in obvious distress. He couldn't stop coughing and he was dry heaving and gagging like I was the morning after I let my friends talk me into raiding Grandma's cabinet full of my grandfather's old liquor. *What is in Muscatel anyway?* Grandma and Sherry tried to help Terry but what help can a mother and sister offer to a man stricken with Leukemia? It was obvious that running the race was too much for him. I believe that at the time of the last race, Terry knew he was going to die soon. I guess getting sick for him was similar to getting old for me. His body quit on him before his brain did. And it isn't until you take that first swing at a rival and miss, come down in pain from a failed jump shot that used to be like water or run and lose a damn race against your slower little brother, that you realize you are on the downside of your time on Earth.

I remember standing in the kitchen with my mother. It was just the two of us in there but she spoke to me like her words were confidential when she said, *"Terry needs a bone marrow transplant. We all need to get checked to see if we are a match. If none of us match, he is going to die. The doctor said he only has six months to live."* Probably three months after that conversation with my mother, my Uncle Terry was dead. He was the first person in my life that I loved and had to watch die. I am eerily used to it now but back then his death was really hard on me.

Once again, it is the memory of a phone call that sets my pain in motion. It was just my sister Joan and I at home when the call came in. I answered it and my Great Aunt Shannon's voice came softly over the line. *"Hey John Marc... I hate to have to tell you this but Terry passed away a little while ago. I am so sorry."*

I held it together and then looked over to Joan and said, *"Terry just died."* Then I flipped the chair over and we both sat there in the living room and cried.

It was hours before all of my family arrived at the house from the hospital. I remember it was after dark and I wasn't asleep but in my bed when Howard and John entered my room. Howard said, *"Old Terry White's gone, Marc."* I could tell that they both suffered immensely through their initial moments of despair. Although the tracks of their tears were still visible like footprints in the sand, their faces seemed to show only acceptance and quiet remembrance as they sat down side by side on the other bed in my room. I called it my room but everyone else in my family always called it *"The Boy's Room."* That room has always been the bedroom for the boys, even back when Howard, Terry and John were children. So there I sat in *"The Boy's Room"* with two of the big boys, each one of us greatly missing the third. I thought to myself as I watched my Uncle Howard start to cry again, *"What about Grandma?"*

My grandmother was in the house somewhere and of all the people that were in there that night she was the one that I didn't want to see. I didn't want to see Grandma because Terry's sickness put her on a roller coaster ride that lasted for months. And at the end of the line the rollercoaster jumped the tracks and crashed into the water below. The good days. The bad ones. The days we thought Terry would be okay. The times when we worried that he would die. Each one of them had an affect on my grandmother and was, I'm sure, the worst experience of her life. And that is saying something, considering the fact that I am talking about Mattie Irene White. A woman who has suffered through enough pain to fill fifty books. My kids allowed me to have a taste of what she experienced. I had to fear losing both of my children but my experience amounted to just a sip of the pain my grandmother was forced to swallow like gallons of cold King Syrup. And that little sip that I swallowed almost choked the life out of me. And my baby didn't die at the end of the ride either. Mattie Irene White was a strong lady.

I begged and prayed many times for Terry to be spared but it is Leukemia that I am talking about. Plus he went down so quickly that I should have known that he was going to die. Terry knew. I let church and the Bible make me believe that God was going to spare Terry's life. Sitting there in the back of the church, listening to Reverend Smith every Sunday and I do mean *every* Sunday; I was forced to believe that my Uncle Terry was going to beat that disease. That God would answer my prayers. Our prayers. That God wanted Terry to be fine. Then when Terry didn't beat it, I was told that his death was God's will. Too many mixed messages and more proof to me that people don't know shit.

I remember the last time Terry and I talked. It was during the NFL football strike and I was laying down watching a rerun of a football game. He walked into my room and sat down on the on the other bed, almost in the same spot where Howard and John sat on the night he died. He had lost so much weight that his cheekbones looked like they were going to poke right through his skin. Our conversation wasn't anything really deep or moving even though I know now that he was saying goodbye. If I hadn't been so blinded by faith then I would have known that it was the last time that we were ever going to talk. I would have made sure our conversation was more profound. I would have told him that I loved him.

Terry took a turn for the worst not long after our conversation in my room. He made one last trip to the hospital. He was tired and ready to die when he heard Death knocking at his door. He didn't run and hide in the closet like my Uncle John used to do when the police showed up at the house looking for him. Instead my Uncle Terry accepted Death's invitation and pulled out all of the needles, cables and wires that were connecting him to the hospital equipment and he went willingly into his next life.

When he died, my grandmother was next to him and she crawled on top of his body and just laid there.

I hate the thought of that moment and the pictures that I have drawn of it in my mind make me feel ill as I sit here. I picture her pleading unsuccessfully with him to stop as he ripped the needles out of his arms and her stare as she watched him take his last breath. I picture the look on her face as the realization of his demise sank in. I can see her slipping her tiny feet into the metal railings of the bed and slowly and painfully pulling herself on top of him. I picture her climbing up on that hospital bed, with tears in her eyes and a stake in her heart, desperately wanting to feel the last minutes of warmth of her favorite son and it makes me sick.

It was over. My grandmother had been weighed. She had been measured. And at the end of the day her strength was not found wanting. I thank my God for that. Like the little boy soldiers of Sierra Leone, she endured an immense amount of loss. But she kept her feet moving on through the thick forests of life as if nothing happened. The twelve year old killers that waged war in the forests of Sierra Leone did not have the time to mourn the dead. And although my Uncle Terry's death hit my grandmother hard, like a bullet from one of the young African's AK-47's, the shot only caused her to lose step for a minute. Because it wasn't long before she was back in stride and ready to lead her family. It had been her job ever since her husband went down and she was not about to fail us.

9

> *"Choose rather to be strong of soul than strong of body."*
> *-Pythagoras*

My grandmother should have had either an easier or shorter life. But then again, maybe if her life was easier or shorter then more of the rest of us might not be here. There might not have been as many great-grandchildren running around houses all over the east coast if she had checked out earlier. But when I really think about it, even a few extra great-grandchildren don't seem worth the price she had to pay for the cards that she was dealt in life.

If pain, heartache and loss were a Visa card, then my grandmother's would be platinum. And it would also be maxed out. Shirley Caesar said, *"When you add it all up, the full cost of real love is no charge."* My grandmother loved that song and proved its chorus to be true for all of her children and grandchildren. But even though there was no charge for the advice and the knowledge and the cost of my college; there were still debts to be paid. For the price of life is death and Mr. Reaper doesn't accept checks.

If I were to count the number of times that my grandmother had to sit in the front center pew at our church in Rectortown or deal with Mr. Joynes or some other mortician, I would need a calculator. She buried her husband. She buried her children. She buried a grandchild. She buried her parents. She buried brothers and sisters. That is just too much blood, pain and graveside seats for a little old lady that never hurt a fly. If there is a Heaven and she is not there then there is a serious problem.

My grandfather trained race horses for Paul Mellon at Rokeby Stables and because of that we had two houses when I was little. We had our family house in Rectortown with the wood burning stove and no running water. And then we had a house on a horse farm outside of Middleburg, VA that had wall to wall carpet, air conditioning and two bathrooms. It was like night and day.

On April 17, 1975, the day my grandfather died, my grandmother was in Rectortown at the family house. I was in Middleburg, down at the stables with my grandfather and Uncle John. I was four. I don't remember much about my grandfather except that he was a big and strong man. I don't remember his voice or what his hands felt like as he hoisted me in the air. What I do remember is the sight of two horses, one brown, one black, charging across our back yard like the wild mustangs of yesteryear. Neither of them had a rider and they ran like escaped convicts with freedom just a stride away. And apples, I remember a wooden bowl full of Golden Delicious apples with light brown freckles on them.

When his heart seized up and gave out on him, my grandfather was walking two horses from the paddock into the stables. One was brown. One was black. My Uncle John was the first to get to him and he found his father lying on his back at the entrance to the stables. I was so young and am amazed that I remember this all so clearly but I do. I bet I could go back to those stables today and point out the exact spot where he fell. *Death has always had the power to vividly and permanently sear recollections into my memory like a ranch hand's branding iron.* John was panic stricken and his screams for help are what brought my mother sprinting down the driveway like Flo-Jo. For a few seconds I was alone with my grandfather as he lay on the ground dead or dying. John had sprinted off to get a cup of water. I remember being about ten feet from his still body and shocked at how large his stomach seemed as he lay flat on his back with both of his arms at his sides.

By the time Ma got down to us, John was back with the water. He was about to pour it on my grandfather's face. I guess he saw that in a movie somewhere. Throw some water on the face of someone that passed out and they snap right out of it. He stood over his father with a cup of cold water held in the hand of his outstretched arm. At the last second, right before the first drop could fall, he looked at us. My mother and I. I think he realized that the water was not going to do the trick. And after he looked at us, he stopped, threw the cup of water on the ground and dropped to his knees in tears knowing full well that his father was dead.

The ambulances came anyway and as always, the kids were whisked away to avoid seeing anything that might haunt them for the rest of their lives. *Good job there.* My sisters and I were taken to a neighbor's house. While standing on the front stoop of our neighbor's house, we were each given a yellow apple by a nice white lady. We ate them as we watched the farm hands chase after the two escaped horses and as the ambulance headed down the driveway with our grandfather in the back.

Grandma was at work when her husband was departing this life. She used to get dropped off at the house in Rectortown and then my grandfather would go pick her up in the evenings and bring her to the other house on the farm. Not that evening. Not anymore evenings. Arthur was the name of the man that felt it was his duty to inform my grandmother of her husband's death. Honestly and even though he is most likely either dead or definitely very old right now, I would still like to find him and put my foot dead in his ass. My grandmother felt that way too. He drove to our house in Rectortown, walked in and said, *"Mattie you need to come with me."* And when she refused he screamed, *"Dammit Mattie! Boots is dead! You need to come with me!"* That is how she learned of the loss of her husband. Boots was my grandfather's nickname and I never heard my grandmother use anything else to call him even twenty years after he was gone. Years later I heard her tell the story about how she was informed of my grandfather's passing. She said that she got weak in the knees when she heard the news and Arthur, that asshole of a man, actually had to grab her to keep her from hitting the floor. I know that there is really no easy way to tell a person that someone they love is dead but that man hurt my grandmother and was completely out of line. She deserved better. And Arthur deserves an ass whipping.

I can remember my grandfather's death but not his funeral. I have seen lots of pictures from it though. They each make me think the same thing. And that is I don't want any photos of my dead body. No pictures snapped by a loved one during a grief-filled momentary loss of sanity to be stuck in a photo album and left laying around to scar one of my nieces or little cousins for life. Who would want to see that picture anyway? Surely not anyone that loved and missed me. What if one of my babies saw it? It is bad enough that I have death running across my mind like Jilly from Philly but to actually have a visual reminder that I can hold in my hand just feels wrong to me.

Just like my grandfather, there were pictures of Shawn lying in her casket. And I do remember her funeral. At least one part of it. And what is crazy is that I wasn't even two years old. Unfortunately neither was Shawn. She died before Granddaddy and I know that I shouldn't remember her funeral but once again, I do. I even remember her death. I was there.

Back in the day our yard was always filled with children and I remember there being a lot of family at the house that day. We were all playing on the homemade basketball court on the other side of our driveway. The basketball court was set on a slightly more elevated piece of land than the rest of the property. This created a small embankment along the left side of the driveway. If you were pulling into our yard, the court was on the left and the embankment gave it the illusion that the basketball court was raised like a small stage. Even as I sit here more than thirty years later I can still clearly see the basketball rolling down the embankment and into the driveway with Shawn chasing right after it. My Uncle Terry had his car parked in the driveway parallel with the basketball court. Just as he started backing up the ball went rolling down the bank. He never saw her. Shawn ran down the embankment, bent down to pick up the ball and the car went rolling right over her. Fortunately I don't remember the sound of her tiny body breaking under the weight of the car. I also don't remember the ambulance in the yard or what my Uncle Terry said or did upon realizing what had just happened. What I do remember is my Aunt Sherry, Shawn's mother, as she came running out of the house with Grandma right on her heels. She was screaming like a banshee. I don't remember anything else about that incident and I am thankful for that because I know it was one of my family's darkest days.

At Shawn's funeral I was too little to see inside the casket. And I remember being lifted from behind and raised into the air by someone to look down on the face of a fallen angel. I would bet my life that her funeral was a horrible experience and I am so thankful that I only have the one memory of it. Now that I am a father it is easier for me to imagine what Sherry and James must have felt losing their daughter. I said imagine. Because if I had to actually experience the loss of my child in such a tragic way I don't think I would be able to deal.

10

"There's no tragedy in life like the death of a child. Things never get back to the way they were."

-Dwight David Eisenhower

Losing your child is obviously the worst thing that can happen to any parent. But I feel that watching your child slowly wither away from an illness or disease is easier on the mind, body and soul than having your kid snatched away from you suddenly or tragically. From watching my mother slowly slip away from me, I believe that I have acquired a parallel understanding of how it might feel to watch one of my children die from an illness or disease. But if I wanted to know what it felt like to lose one of my children, actually both of my children, suddenly or tragically, all I would have to do is ask Sherry.

My Aunt Sherry spent several weeks in 1985, way out in Hagerstown, Maryland in the hospital after a really bad car accident. My whole family went on a trip to Hershey Park. I was fourteen at the time and was at that age where I felt I was grown and could do my own thing. So I stayed home. On their way back home the car that Sherry was driving was hit almost head-on by a man speeding away from the police on the wrong side of the highway. In the car with Sherry was her husband, James and her two sons, Poogie and Deon. Our cousin Pinky was in back with the kids as well. Pinky and the kids were shaken and bruised. James' leg was really banged up and I believe broken. But Sherry was really hurt. I went to see her in the hospital. She was unconscious and her face was cut up and swollen. It was a horrible accident, I hate calling it an accident because the cops were chasing a drunk driver down the wrong side of the highway. I feel the other driver and the police officer caused the crash because they both had to know it was coming. *How the hell are you going to chase a speeding drunk driver down the wrong side of the road in the middle of the night?* Sherry probably should've died in the accident but she fought through it, survived and beat Death back into its black hole. She had won. But after she lost another child, suddenly and tragically, I bet she wished she had lost.

If my family were a Walt Disney movie, I would be The Big Bad Wolf. But Deon would have been, without question, Bambi. The only thing he ever hurt was his big brother, Poogie and I'm sure that Poogie deserved it. Deon represented the softer side of a man. He couldn't help it. He tried to be tough. He tried to be bad sometimes but it just wasn't in him. That is why I think he idolized me so much as being bad was definitely in me.

I remember one time I was sitting in the back of our church. From where I sat I could see the back of Deon's head. I thought to myself, *"When I have children, I hope I have a little boy that looks like Deon and a little girl that looks like Toye Gaines."* Sherry and James' genes hooked up real good on Deon. He was always cute little boy and grew into a handsome young man.

Growing up Deon was the *"tagalong."* He was younger than all of us by more than five years but couldn't wait to hang out with the fellas. He wasn't that much of an athlete but he loved being at the basketball court with us just feeling like one of the boys. I could tell that it was something he lived for.

When he got older and we finally let him hang I think he wanted to prove to all of us that he could be *"down,"* but the night usually ended with everything coming right back *"up."* I don't think I have owned a vehicle that Deon didn't throw up in on the way home from some party.

I worried about Deon, though. I worried about the type of man he was going to grow up to be. I worried if someone would one day take full advantage of him and his kindness. I felt he was open to that. I also worried about how he would do in school. But he made it and graduated from high school on time. He had a speech problem that made him hard to understand sometimes but I loved him so much that I never asked him to repeat himself and learned to understand what he was saying. I think his speech got worse after he got hit by the car. Oh snap! I never mentioned that when he was ten, Deon got hit by a car driven by his own father, in his own driveway. Insane, I know. The parallels on this one are astounding.

After I saw Deon, lying unconscious and still, on pavement so hot that the tar bubbled, I just felt like Sherry and James could never catch a break. This was awful.

We were sitting at my grandmother's kitchen table when all of the sudden our neighbor, Wendell, kicked in the door like Biggie and his .44 and as calmly as he could, said, *"Sherry, James just ran over Deon with the car. He is lying in the street in front of the house. You better get up there."*

Sherry screamed, *"Oh, God No!"*

I know she was thinking or trying not to think, about Shawn and what happened many years ago, because once again there she was sitting in her mother's house when someone ran in and told her to come quick because her child got hit by a car. What else was she going to think about? Two kids with two cars and two family members behind the wheel two separate times. Whoa.

At the time Sherry, James and the kids lived two houses up from the church, which made it easy walking distance from Grandma's house. On this day it was easy sprinting distance.

In an instant the house cleared, cars sat empty in the driveway and we were all running up the street. We raced past Aunt Will's house, some with no shoes on our feet. We flew past Uncle Smitty's yard with sounds of the ambulance screaming in the distance. Our little Deon's welfare, at the time our only care. In between my own heaving breaths I thought, *"Please God, don't let him die."* As I made it past the church, I saw Poogie with tears in his eyes. The tar on the road bubbled from the blazing summer heat. Face down and covered with sweat, Deon lay motionless in the street.

The brush next door to Sherry and James' house had grown up way too high. It made pulling out of their driveway very dangerous. Sometimes you were halfway in the street before you could tell if the coast was clear. And when it wasn't you had better know how to back up real fast. On this day James was pulling his extra large station wagon into the driveway. Clark Griswold comes to mind when I think about how big that old station wagon was. At the same time James was pulling into the driveway, Poogie and Deon were flying out of the driveway on their bicycles. Deon crashed head first into the windshield, bounced off the hood and landed in the street.

My eyes scanned the scene. I noticed that Deon's bike was crumpled like an empty soda can. The driver-side of the windshield was shattered and the cracks spread out like a spider's web. That meant that James was only a foot away from the face of his son as it smashed into the windshield. I want to know desperately if the two of them made eye contact in the brief instant before he crashed into his son but I will never ask.

Deon was still and looked dead. He had a small patch of hair missing from the back of his head that wasn't bleeding but looked unnatural and was very unnerving. It was so hot. I just wanted to pour some cold water on him. I wanted to pick him up but we knew that we shouldn't move him. Then the ambulance and fire trucks showed up and blocked the road.

Back then I had a really good friend named Angie Soaper. Every member of Angie's family except her mother, were Marshall Volunteer Firefighters from middle school all the way to adulthood. I remember seeing Angie as she followed her older brother and sisters off of the truck and saw the lifeless little body in the street. She looked up and saw me and my appearance of despair and shot me a look of concern that has stuck with me ever since. I hope she is doing well.

Gently, two of the Soaper sisters rolled Deon over onto the wooden stretcher board. His body was limp, his eyes were closed and I thought he was dead. They slid him into the back of the ambulance and once again I was forced to watch as an ambulance rolled away, not only with its sirens blaring but also with another loved one in the back.

Deon was flown by helicopter to Fairfax Hospital where he would recover from his run-in with the station wagon. This story and my new way of thinking makes me wonder if that day in the street was really supposed to be his day. I mean his day to go to God. I wonder if it was in the cards for Deon to die that day by whoever was driving the next car that was coming up the street. It just so happened that the next car was driven by his own father. I wonder if Deon was dead in the minutes that it took for the ambulance to get there. We didn't touch him, so who knows for real? I wonder if, when Deon's *"Watcher"* notified God about the accident. If God looked at him like Samuel L. Jackson used to look at his victims in Pulp Fiction right before he struck them down with *great vengeance and furious anger.* And instead of laying His wrath upon the *"Watcher,"* God laid his mercy on our family and gave Deon more time. But not a lot.

Deon was ten when he got hit by that car. When he survived I thought it was smooth sailing on out for him. Once again life proved me wrong. I thought that since he went one-on-one with a station wagon and won, the rest of life would be a slam dunk for him. It wasn't. He made it through high school but his speech got worse as he got older. And so did his friends. I do remember Sherry saying something good about one of them. But she also believes that some of the others broke into their house. I said that I worried about Deon when he was younger but as he got older, I really worried about him.

In the end, a hotdog did what over one thousand pounds of metal and glass couldn't. It took Deon's life. Knowing Deon like I did, I know he was scared when he couldn't cough that chunk of meat out of his throat. I know he panicked and was stricken with fear as he crashed around the room and fell to the floor without enough air in his lungs. He went out scared and that is what fucks me up.

I think that after God saw Deon lying in the street that day many years ago and then looked down the road at his panicked mother sprinting up the street, He decided to postpone Deon's departure. Even though it was Deon's scheduled *"date,"* God could not do that to Sherry and James again. To lose another child in the exact same manner would have devastated them both and possibly interfered with them completing each of their own tasks. But rules are rules and Deon still had to go. His time was up and whatever his task was, it was completed before the age of ten. The next fifteen years were just gravy for him. And us.

Grandma died before Deon and I am glad she didn't have to bury him. Deon was special to her and seeing him in that casket would have ripped open wounds that, although scabbed over and appearing to be healed, were still so deep that they had to ache from time to time. God is merciful and He gave her a pass on Deon because in her lifetime she had seen enough.

11

"A little more matriarchy is what the world needs and I know it. Period. Paragraph."

-Dorothy Thompson

My Great Uncle John called me yesterday and asked me if I could come over and give him a hand.

"Marc I really need your help. It will only take a few minutes. I need you to hold a ladder for me."

I thought to myself as I listened to him on the phone, *"A ladder? Why the hell does he need me to hold a ladder? He shouldn't be up on any ladder. Yikes."*

The cause of my concern comes from the fact that my Uncle John is the last of my grandmother's brothers and sisters. He is too old to do a lot of the things that he does but he is stubborn as a mule and his age is the last thing that is going to stop him from doing what he wants.

It was only a few weeks back that I was visiting him in the hospital concerned that his heart was going to give out on him. He spent a week in the hospital and could not wait to get out. I sat there in his hospital room and listened to him talk about getting out of the hospital like I talked about getting out of prison. He feels like when people make a fuss about him that he is somehow a burden. He never seems to realize that we love being around him. All he wanted and talked about was getting back to his apartment. He had to know that he was going to have to stay with family at least until we were sure he was going to be okay. He had serious problems with his neighbors everywhere he lived and that plus the fact that he has a very big gun always caused me concern. There were several times I walked into his apartment and saw that big Magnum lying on the table like a cobra ready to strike. I just knew that I was going to get the call late one night that he shot somebody with it. Desiree even saw it once.

"Daddy. I saw Uncle John's gun."

"Did you touch it?" I asked with tremendous fear and fright.

"No but I saw it. It was wrapped up in a sweatshirt between the seats and it was big. Really big."

Okay, so back to my ladder story. My Uncle John is staying with my cousin Liecy in Fort Washington, Maryland while he gets his health in order. So I make the ten minute trip over to her house. I pull up and my Uncle John is sitting in the passenger seat of his car with one foot hanging out and a cigarette in dangling from his lips, looking pissed off. I expected to go inside to hang a star on the Christmas tree or string some lights around the inside of the house. That is what I expected. But of course I was wrong.

I stood in front of the large two story house thinking okay maybe he needs me to string some lights along the lower edge of the roof. But I could see the lights dangling from the top of the house. The very top. The highest parts that were easily thirty feet off the ground. Some moron thought it was wise and festive-looking to use three-inch pieces of gray duct tape to string Christmas lights along the roof of the house. For the sake of the story his name is Mr. Apple and Mr. Apple is an idiot. I can tell this chapter is going to take a while because I can't stop laughing long enough to type. I know it is not nice to call people names but Mr. Apple leaves me no choice. If he had checked the news at least once before he taped the lights to the house, he would have known that a rainstorm was coming.

My cousin Liecy definitely gets the Christmas spirit and she turns her home into a Christmas wonderland. So when she got up to leave that morning and saw large strands of lights sagging and falling from her house, she freaked out. She called back into the house and asked my Uncle John what he could do, obviously not knowing that he was definitely going to do something.

With a box full of white clips in his hand, he pointed at the dangling lights. He said to me with a sound of disgust and a look of disbelief, *"Marc. Look at this shit."*

I looked up and saw the lights dangling and falling from different parts of the roof and knew instantly that this was going to be a chapter in my book but still was shocked at what came next.

As I followed him around the house, he was stuffing the clips into his pockets. We went up the back stairs to the patio that is about twelve to fourteen feet off the ground. The ladder was sitting on the patio, situated in a way that let me know he was planning on going up on the top of the house. The very top. It had just rained, the ladder was rickety, he was just out of the damn hospital and he is old. I was scared shitless.

I surveyed the scene with the wet deck and rickety and rusty ladder and said, *"Uncle John. I know you are not planning on going up on that roof to fix those lights, are you?*

"Who else is going to do it, Marc?"

I thought to myself as I looked up at how high the roof was from the ground, *"Well I know I'm not going to do it. How am I going to talk him out of this shit?"*

I followed him as he angrily marched around the house, up the stairs and straight to the ladder.

I said to him, *"Man, let me go up there and do it."*

All I got back was slow fire. *"Damnit Marc. Shut the fuck up. I got it."*

I pleaded unsuccessfully, *"I know you got it Uncle John but it is wet. Let me do it. Please."*

Once again I got a verbal ass whipping, *"Marc. Hold the damn ladder and shut the hell up. I got it!"*

I pleaded with him for minutes that seemed like hours. I could tell that I was pissing him off. It got to a point where I worried that if I upset him any more then his chances of falling off the house would increase. So I gave in and just held the ladder because I knew that he was going back up on the roof and there was nothing I could do about it.

I nervously watched as he slowly climbed up on the roof. He got up there and scooted over to the very edge and started clipping the Christmas lights to the edge of the roof. Less than a slip, all it would have taken for him to go crashing to the ground was a medium-sized gust of wind. I kept nagging him. I couldn't help it.

"Uncle John. Please. Come down. Let me do it."

"Marc, it is wet up here. I don't want you to get dirty. I'm already keeping you from your shopping. Just be quiet and let me finish. As a matter of fact, get down on the ground and tell me what it looks like."

"Uncle John, I'm not worried about getting my jeans dirty. I'm worried about what the family is going to think of me when you fall off the damn roof."

"Marc, just get down on the ground and tell me if the lights are hanging right."

It wasn't until I got down to the bottom of the stairs that I could fully appreciate just how high off the ground my Uncle John was. I was scared shitless all over again. I don't want to say exactly how much my cousin paid Mr. Apple to tape the lights to her house but I know that I will never ever forget how much she paid Mr. Apple to tape the lights to her house. I will always remember it because my Uncle John kept repeating the number over and over again. And each time he looked down at me and said it, he had the look of a person saying, *"Can you believe that shit?"* As a child he always reminded me of Richard Pryor. And while sitting up there on that roof he had me laughing like I was ten again and secretly listening to one of my Uncle Terry's Richard Pryor albums before Grandma got home from work. He was cracking me up. I stood in the yard looking up at my Uncle John on top of the house and laughed until my stomach hurt. I know the neighbors had to be wondering what was so funny.

"Uncle John, I can't believe someone would tape Christmas lights to the house. That is a first for me."

"Don't forget Marc, he got paid $$$ to do this shit."

"Uncle John, I am in the wrong business."

He huffed and said, *"You think? She ain't the only one Marc, Mr. Apple got a couple of houses on the street. I told him that he could make a lot of money with that lift machine that he had."*

"Hold up Uncle John. You mean Mr. Apple actually had a machine that helped him do this shit?"

"Oh Marc. He had a big old machine with a boom on it that put him right up to the edge of the roof. And he got paid $$$ to do it. Don't forget that."

I laughed, *"You won't let me."*

I watched as he neatly clipped the strands of lights along the side of the house, working his way from the back to the front. I was stressing about what he was going to do when he got to the corner. He works on the Woodrow Wilson Bridge Project and his job requires that he have no fear of heights. He proved it to me as he navigated the strand of lights along the corner of the roof with ease. I breathed a sigh of relief and with each clip that he placed on the roof I became more comfortable with him being up there in the first place. I was almost amazed at what I was watching. He got halfway across the front of the house when he looked down at me and said, *"Okay Marc, I'm starting to feel a little winded."*

Time to go to work.

"Okay man, come on down. I will finish it up."

I wasn't laughing anymore. I was scared. And I am not talking about of falling. I was scared that my Uncle John would have some sort of heart attack right there on the spot and then what? So I held on to that ladder like it was made of gold as my Uncle John slowly came down and quickly went into supervisor mode. Okay. Uncle John is safe. Now I can worry about falling. I nervously climbed up on the roof and strung the lights exactly the way he ordered me to. Fortunately, I didn't slip, fall and go crashing to my death but I sure thought I was going to. And at the end of it all, the house looked perfect, my Uncle John was safe and I had a story for my book. It was a good day.

I said earlier that my Uncle John feels like he is a burden on everyone and can't understand why we love being around him. I'm sure each family member has their own reason but mine is simple. His face. I love being around him because of his face. I look at him and I see Aunt Shannon. I see Aunt Thelma, Uncle Mack and Uncle Buddy. I see Grandma. Especially when he is mad at me.

My grandmother had eight brothers and sisters. Their personalities and lives spanned the whole spectrum. In amongst the nine of them were years of tales of life and death that couldn't be completely told in nine hundred books. If she were capable when she was alive, my Great Aunt Dease could have written a classic *"Country Mouse-City Mouse"* tale twisted with pimps, drugs and dealers of the disco days and how the effects of them took her out of the race many years before she was ready. She spent the last twenty years of her life in a nursing home unable to talk, walk or function on her own. The doctors say that it was Multiple Sclerosis that put her in that state. My uncle says different. He blames drugs and a white pimp from back in the day. I know my Great Uncle Tom had stories to tell. He ran from horses and alcoholism in the country and found horses, alcoholism and death in New York City. He was struck down as an old man by an automobile while crossing a busy city street. Those are just two of the books that could have been written between the nine of them. I'm only willing to put my immediate family's business in the street and I try to be underwhelming with that but I don't think it would do any harm to say that the rest of my grandmother's brothers and sisters had a few interesting novels that could have been penned as well.

I wonder what my grandmother's book would have been like. I bet it would have been awesome. I know she would have mentioned Terry and Shawn's death and that strange night in the middle of the street. And I am positive that the pages on my grandfather would have flowed like the Mighty Mississippi with words of love and terms of endearment. And when she finally got up the nerve to write about how she felt losing him, I know it would have made the reader's eyes well up with tears. Sometimes when thinking about how I am now writing the stories that I know she would have written makes me wonder whose book I am writing. Mine or hers?

I was at work when I got the call. One of Chrisi's friends called to tell me that my grandmother was at the Alexandria Hospital and I should hurry up and get there. I remember leaving out of the America Online lobby in a flash. Now that I think about it, I sure did drive a lot of *"scared shitless"* miles in that old green Suburban.

My grandmother never had what I would call pretty feet. In fact they were downright ugly. I can remember her lying on the sofa with my Aunt Phyl clipping her toenails and laughing as those things shot clean across the room like mini boomerangs. It was funny because Phyl jumped like a kid lighting a firecracker with a short fuse each time she clipped a nail. But that Christmas night when we looked down at her feet and saw that one of her toes was completely black, we knew that it was more than a case of ugly feet.

We took her to the hospital and found out that she had circulation problems and the toe would have to be amputated. From there things spiraled out of control. It seemed like every time we'd turn around the doctor was cutting off a piece of my grandmother. The doctor finally put his saw down when he got just below my grandmother's knee and when he was done he left her with a *"two-piece dark meat."* A leg and a thigh.

I know the physical pain that she suffered was excruciating. And after all the emotional weights that she had to carry over the years, to see her writhing in pain in that hospital bed made me sick. I remember a feeling of contempt for God during the period that my grandmother was dying. A deep one.

I remember thinking as I sped down I-495 to the hospital, *"What is going on? Grandma was doing good."* And she had been. Even though she was missing a leg, she was still Grandma. Nothing about her changed other than she was not as mobile as she once was. It was hard to look at her at first but after I realized that everything else was the same, it was like back to normal.

I pulled up to the hospital and I saw Phyl and Howard outside. Howard was crying so I knew things weren't good.

Phyl said, *"Mom had a stroke, Marc."*

"How is she?" I asked.

Phyl smiled and said, *"She's alive. And you know Mom is a fighter."*

Her smile didn't seem genuine and she sounded a bit too positive about things. Also, she didn't cry and that told me that she was hiding the facts and her own uncertainties. She was trying to be strong. She directed me to the room where my grandmother was and when I saw the truth with my own eyes, I wished she had kept the room location a secret right along with her real feelings and concerns.

I walked into the hospital room. Chrisi was in there holding Grandma's hand. She said, *"There's Marc. He made it."*

Grandma was facing Chrisi when I walked into the room. After Chrisi announced to her that I was there, she turned very unnaturally to look in my direction. I could tell that she wanted to say something. But she couldn't. All that came out were grunts and groans. I was sickened. The fact that she couldn't talk made her struggle that much harder and she rolled around in that bed silently screaming at me that she was going to be fine. Her eyes said to me, *"Don't worry. I'm ok. You go be the man that I always knew you could be."* It was one of the hardest things I have ever had to witness and it was only seconds before the tears started to puddle on the floor. This was it. This was the moment that our family had been secretly dreading for our entire lives. She was leaving us. Grandma had been involved in many fights over the years and she was knocked down many many times. But she always got back up. Always. Life was so hard on her, we all knew that. But her strength was so evident to all of us that watching her get back up had almost become a given. We all had gotten so used to her getting up and fighting on that we just expected her to overcome anything even a massive stroke. But this time was different, at least for me it was. I knew that this time the ref was going to get to ten even if it took him a month to get there.

…8, 9, 10! Ding! Ding! Ding!

I complained in my first book about how Hollywood doesn't always portray an accurate view of family life. But after Grandma died I learned that sometimes they do get it right out there in L.A. I don't know how many of you ever saw the movie *"Soul Food,"* but if ever a movie accurately portrayed how a single death can disintegrate a family, that one did. Just like in the movie with Big Mama, when my grandmother died it left us leaderless. Leaderless and wandering in a thousand different directions at a time when decisions had to be made. Leaderless at a time when we needed a leader the most.

My Uncle Howard is the oldest of my grandmother's children and I guess he figured that the spot was naturally his for the taking. Several discussions ended with just his foot being put down. Some of us didn't like that. Especially some of us grandkids. I understood that it was more than just their mother that my aunts and uncles were burying and that is why I didn't try to voice my opinions or concerns often. But I remember feeling totally excluded from the whole process and it angered me. And more anger was the last thing I needed during that time. We held family meetings to decide what was what. It was during the family meetings that I first saw the separation that was coming. It was during these meetings that I saw the glue first start to weaken. It was like lines were drawn and sides were chosen, within the damn family. It was a tough time.

I blamed The Man Upstairs for this all happening and I can remember feeling a lot of deep-seated resentment back then. And 99.9% of it was aimed directly at God. I didn't know if it was right to feel like I did but I missed my grandmother and the pain and frustration became so overwhelming that I stood up in church and fessed up to it publicly and live at my grandmother's wake.

I was younger and not yet set on my religious views when my grandmother died. So I didn't realize that it was simply her time. Her race had been run. Her task obviously complete. So with that being said, in a very well cultivated moment of misinformation I just pointed an angry finger at God. As far as my young mind was concerned, God let that shit happen and I was furious. And I am not just talking about Grandma dying. I blamed God for the slow disintegration of my family that I watched ever so closely.

I remember telling Rocky, my cousin the preacher, Rodney's father that I felt like I should say something. I believe he thought I meant some heartfelt words about my grandmother. I mean I knew that would be part of my *"speech"* because I loved my grandmother so. But I mainly felt the strange need to voice my concerns about what I was witnessing within my family and how I felt that if God was in control then God was responsible. And according to my thinking at the time, what better place to do that than at church? In a way I felt that standing up in church and pointing my finger at God was blasphemous but I did it suffering through the misery of a man who had just had his heart ripped from him. And I did it with the hopes that surely someone from the congregation would rush the answers over to me. They never came and I went home that night filled with questions and doubts, prepared for the funeral the next day and let the seeds of a new relationship with a new God finally begin to sprout.

That is the only thing positive that has come out of my grandmother's death for me. Nothing else. But in a selfish way it is enough. I am happy with my relationship with God now. Very happy. That wouldn't have happened without her death. She had to die in order for me to be able to question so much of what she believed deeply. She had to die because I wouldn't have dared done it while she was alive and able to smack the shit out of me.

My grandmother, Mattie Irene White fought a good fight and we put that on her obituary. The roads she ran were bumpy, filled with potholes and broken glass and led her head-on into the midst of the world's worst agonies. She finished on her back but she finished and that was after running miles with only one leg. She left with more than she came with and she left more behind than she was ever given. I hope she found Heaven.

12

"Every person I work with knows something better than me. My job is to listen long enough to find it and use it."

-Jack Nichols

I've found Heaven right here in the city. Therefore, when I die I want my funeral to be held at the Armed Forces Retirement Home of Washington. Yes, The Old Soldier's Home. I want to have my funeral service at work and led by Pastor Goodloe. Crazy, I know. But I love that place as it is where I feel loved. And I want my shiny silver casket to be lain in deep center of the softball field so when the mourners come, they can look past my casket and witness the view that I have as I walk the path from the Scott Building down to the King Health Center. The trees look as if they were placed with precision and care as they sit down comfortably on rolling hills and at times the scene makes me feel as though I am alone in a far off countryside. As I walk down the path on a rainy day, the squirrels run up to me checking to see if I have anything for them to eat and when they see that I don't, they drop acorn bombs on my head before continuing their game of hide and seek in the soggy leaves. The birds chirp wet songs of delight and if I could sing, I would join right in with them. Actually sometimes I do but only when I am sure that there is no one else is around.

The world is so fast now. Everyone is rushing here and there, to and fro and all the time flying right by the good life as we blindly chase after a better one. The retirement home slows and calms me down. I live in the hood. It is fast, loud, rude and it never sleeps. It is such a drastic contrast to work, which is always peaceful and quiet. Just like I like things to be. When I travel from home to work it is like going from one world to another. And some days when I pass through the

Eagle Gate, I feel like a ten-year-old passing through those revolving and spinning things at the entrance gates of Kings Dominion.

Don't get me wrong. I still hate getting up and going to work but not for the same reasons as I used to. Now I hate getting up because I feel old in the morning and would rather sleep in or listen to the radio. I sleepwalk through my apartment looking for something to wear trying as hard as I can to figure out what is clean and what is not. *(When the kids come over clean clothes end up in the laundry bag while dirty ones hang in the closet. Go figure.)* I iron my pants and shirt with weary eyes and listen and laugh as the Sports Junkies do their morning thing. I shave, shower, dress and usually get outside just in time to see the A8 Bus pulling off from the bus stop. I never run after it and instead I start off on foot to the metro. That isn't really a bad thing though. I think a lot when I walk and many of the chapters in this book came to life on one of my many treks to the Congress Heights metro station. I tend to make it down the escalator just in time to see the doors to the train close on someone's back. As an installed safety feature, the doors open back up immediately if obstructed. In a brief instant the thought of running down the steps and springing onto the train crosses my mind. But it is just a fleeting notion because I have had many a morning chuckle watching people, so pressed to get to work that they risk the humiliation of getting squeezed in between two closing train doors. Fortunately Stan doesn't micro-manage me, so I never feel compelled to risk an embarrassing train diving episode first thing in the morning in order to get to work on time but they sure are fun to watch. When my train finally arrives, I step on board and hope to find a seat but usually there are none. I am 6'3" which makes me taller than the average Joe but when I stand on the metro train I feel like Andre the Giant. As I stand and look over the passengers of the train I notice that the train is so black. It is the Green Line so the occupants are going to be predominately dark skinned but that is not what I am talking about. I mean black clothes. Black leather jackets and Northfaces. Black suits and sweaters. The whole train is void of any color anywhere, except for me and my big orange jacket. Sometimes I feel like I am sticking out like a sore thumb. If I see a woman standing up, I mug on the man that is seated next to her. Where did all the gentlemen go? If I see someone reading a book and they look friendly enough, I might offer them one of my bookmarks or post cards but usually in the morning I just wait for a seat to free up, sit down, prop my head up against the window and rest for the twenty minutes that it takes to get to my stop. The H8 Bus is the bus that will take me from Georgia Avenue Metro right to the main gate at my job. I call it the Hate Bus because I hate waiting for the damn thing. And I hate watching it fly past me after I am halfway into my uphill walk. I just hate it.

It isn't until I finally get to work that I wake up. I still work with computers and yes I still hate them but dealing with computer problems is a small price to pay in order to everyday be in such a beautiful and historic place and around so many people that I care about.

The people I know that have worked at the home for many more years than me always say, *"You think the home is pretty now? You should've seen it back in the day when Mrs. Kubish used to take care of things. She had flowers all over the place. It was absolutely beautiful."* I am so sorry I missed it.

I spend a large amount of time trying to find the perfect picture that I am going to use on the front of this book. For some reason the sky is important to me so I know that it has to be an outside shot, hopefully on a beautifully clouded day. I also want to include my kids somehow.

The natural beauty of the home has inspired several covers in my mind and is one of the things that make me love my job. But wait, there is more.

I actually get to spend my days walking in the ancient footsteps of President Abraham Lincoln. Some mornings as I stroll past his summer home, I can picture him, standing tall and slim on the deck looking over the city.

Once, I had the opportunity to participate in the First Annual Poetry on the Greene Festival that took place on the front lawn of the Lincoln Cottage. I stood there in the shadow cast by President Lincoln's former home as I stared out over a crowd of many old soldiers and one young one. I felt extremely honored. I thought to myself, *"Wow. Abraham Lincoln once stood where I am standing."*

You have to understand that even though I have written a book, I still don't really take my writing ability as seriously as I guess others might. But when I knew that I would be standing in front of men and women that I greatly admired, I had no choice but take the poetry festival and my writing ability very seriously. I had the option of either reading a poem written by someone else or I could write my own. I chose to write my own.

Our librarian, Mary, had the place set up really nice. It was a warm spring evening with a slight cooling breeze at times. There were rows of chairs lined up facing the Lincoln Cottage. There were tents set up with drinks, fruit cups, cakes and cookies. The event was obviously something special to the residents of the home. Some of the ladies got all dolled up and wore beautiful dresses and the men neatly pressed suits and ties. Considering where I have been and what I have been through, it is not out of the realm of possibility that I would feel completely out of place in a situation like that. But I didn't. Honestly, I felt strangely at home.

After a brief introduction from Mary about Lincoln and how his words were able to cross all boundaries of time and location, the poetry reading began. I sat next to Miss Virginia Sicotte. I can always tell which of the old ladies were really beautiful in their youth. She is definitely one of them. She wrote a poem about her daughter and wore a turquoise colored dress that flowed like rain water after a torrential downpour. I told her that I thought she looked very pretty and asked if she was nervous. She said, *"I'm not nervous. I'm just hot."* Well, I was nervous. And hot. And as I listened to Capt. Avin Forseth, of the U.S. Army Rangers, read the poem, *Disabled*, by the war poet Wilfred Owen. I was really nervous and really hot.

His voice sounded powerful, presidential and almost king-like. He was a soldier and I could tell that he was one of our finest. He wore a burgundy beret and a light green camouflaged uniform. He stood straight up and chest out, just like you would expect a young soldier to do. As he walked up to receive the microphone, I noticed that his right arm seemed to hang just a bit awkwardly. He reached out with his left hand to grab the mike even though that was the hand that he had the poem in. After he grabbed it he then switched the microphone to his right hand and secured it in place. I am so glad he didn't drop it.

He held the poem tightly in his left. Not because he was left handed though. He held it in his left hand because an Iraqi IED took away some of the use his right arm and hand. Being in prison and running the streets, I know a lot of people with bullet holes and stab wounds. But seeing this man, this broken soldier and knowing what I do about what those guys go through over there, I was just floored to be in his presence.

My poem had to come off well. Really well. Watching that soldier's poise up there and imagining him, bleeding on the side of the road in a far off war zone, took away my nervousness and I was ready. I wanted to make him proud. I wanted to make all of the men in attendance that risked their lives so I can be able to sit here and tell my stories proud as well.

Writing my poem was not easy. Well writing it was but figuring out what I was going to write was tough. What would a bunch of old soldiers want to hear from me? What do I have in common with them? Then it came to me. I would write about my trip to work. I would let them see how much respect I had for them in a way that lets them see what I see.

Through My Eyes

I saw the sun shine on the face of a blind boy in the early morning. As he gazed out the windows of a Metro bus through his young eyes glazed over, I wondered what he saw. Were there visions of Hershey bars and Milky Ways and snowball fights on wintry snow days? Was it his mother?

I feel for him and yet he shows no care. His eyes too dull to witness my stare.

Bring out the clowns, God. Please make his life fun. Let joy, love and laughter be his stand-in for the sun. Let the moons of peace and happiness rock him off to sleep. Let him slumber among shooting stars Dear Lord and his soul I beg You keep.

On that same bus I watched the drool of a wino spindle from his lip to his lap. It shimmered in the sunlight like a strand of Charlotte's web. A sight I was happy the blind boy could not see. His clothes tainted with urine and liquor smell his eyes closed to destiny. I wondered what he saw. Did he dream of hope and possibilities or desperation and missed opportunities? Was it his mother?

I feel for him too. But in a different kind of way. He was 50 years old, at least. Plenty of times to have had his say. But when he spoke was it not clearly? Did his voice crack quiver and cuss? What went so wrong in this man's life that he could pass out on the back of this bus? I pray that you keep him God. I pray that you change his life. I pray that you open his eyes Dear Lord so that the bottle is no longer his wife.

I enter through gates protected by eagles and seated high atop their perch, they welcome me with concrete silence as I finally arrive to work. I traverse a ring of yellow tulips, which are guarded by golden cannon, I walk down the path next to the cottage of Lincoln and that is where I found him.

It is there I see, through the leaves of the poplar trees, a gray-haired old soldier sitting in his wheelchair staring aimlessly at the sky. Looking to heaven, through weary eyes that I know have seen men die. I wondered what he saw. Was it war faces twisted in anguish and young men's screams of pain or life as a country boy again enjoying a summer rain? Was it his mother?

The feelings that I have for him ring of honor and admiration. I'm proud to say, "Good Morning, Sir" but he deserves a standing ovation. He has made my hard life easier. He shed blood so I would not. He put his life on the line probably time after time in wars some seem to have forgot. But not me. I read. I listen. I know his wounds aren't healed. I wish I could go back in time and fight along beside him on the front line and act as some sort of shield. A shield between him and the bullets

> and one between him and the pain and if nothing else one to shelter his head from the cold and pouring rain.
>
> He hails from the greatest generation. From an era where pride ranked best. A time when young men in arms showed the world that America was better than the rest.
>
> His time is not long now and he knows his work's near done. He simply lives for simple pleasures like the rising and setting of the sun. And when that sun rises no more and his eyes close for the very last time I hope he knows how much appreciation resides in this heart of mine.

When I finished reading my poem, I actually saw people drying their eyes. Grown men were telling me that my words made their eyes well up with tears. I felt so proud. I only wanted to make those old soldiers proud and I think my desire was reached. So many people were clamoring to tell me how much they enjoyed my poem. Every step I took, someone was shaking my hand or giving me a hug. All I could think about was, *"Do I shake Captain Forseth's hand with my right or do I extend my left hand? I guess my left but that is my weak hand. I don't want him to think I have a girl's grip."*

I have read that you can't go to war, see what is there for you to see and then come back to the States as the same guy. I believe that. I got the feeling from Capt. Forseth that he would give the use of his left arm too if he could be back over there fighting with his brothers. I didn't ask him but that is just the feeling I got from speaking to him. His concern was for his friends.

Captain Forseth brought his sister with him to the Poetry Festival and from her I got a different vibe. From her all I felt was relief. It showed on her face that she was so happy and thankful to have her brother back. Her brother may have wished for more battles but she had him back and she kept him close. He could long for the war and miss its chaos. He could dream about going back but from the outside looking in, the big strong captain was taking orders from someone else now and the war was no longer an option for him. But unfortunately it is still a bloody alternative for so many others.

13

"You're not to be so blind with patriotism that you can't face reality. Wrong is wrong, no matter who does it or says it."

-Malcolm X

I went through a phase of unknown when I was halfway through my first book. I didn't know what I wanted to write. I liked writing poems. I also liked the idea of actually writing a book. So when I felt something I would just write it down. Several thoughts made it into my first book. Others sat untouched and unread until I could find a place for them somewhere else. Some were destined for this book. Years after finishing my first book I am still running across little notes and scraps of paper with random thoughts scribbled down on them while driving or chewing on a cheeseburger somewhere. I found the following document on one of my old hard drives, it was titled Article and after reading it I found my thoughts to be foretelling and decided to use it in this book.

11/26/2002

To Whom It May Concern:

We are living in an age where patriotism and allegiance to our nation is a must. In my personal opinion, war is definitely not necessary but I know that it is coming. It is evident and only just a short distance away. Now is not the time for discrimination of any beings. We as a country must learn to accept all of our people, whether they are convicted felons who have made and paid for their mistakes or law-abiding citizens working their asses off to ink out a modest living. We must appreciate everything that any American has to offer.

I have been at war my entire adult life and I am tired. I am tired of fighting with the System just to survive its daily discrepancies. I'm tired of fighting just to be able to somehow fit in. The one thing that I do not need is another war. Especially one that may jeopardize the safety of my children. And definitely not because one man says that it's the right thing to do.

The following quote has been attributed to Julius Caesar but its origin has not been proven to be historically accurate. Even so, the wording alone strikes me as inquisitive and its meaning hits home even more so with the status of our nation as it exists today.

"Beware the leader who bangs the drums of war to whip the citizenry into patriotic fervor. For patriotism is indeed a double-edged sword. It both emboldens the blood just as it narrows the mind. When the drums of war have reached a fever pitch and the blood boils with hate and the mind has closed, the leader will have no need in seizing the rights of the citizenry. Rather the citizenry infused with fear and blinded by patriotism will offer up all of their rights into the leader and gladly so. How do I know? For this what I have done and I am Caesar."

Spoken by Caesar or not, these words force me to declare, with no malice in my heart, that I will not fight in or lay down my life for your oil wars. I will not support them and I will not let my children support them. I firmly state this with no equivocation or deception. If you want to see me fight, then let's go to war on homelessness and poverty in America. If you want me to put my hands up and throw them like Mike Tyson used to, then let's go to war with illegal immigration and education, in America. Let's go to war with everything within our country's boundaries that fight to keep the little American man down on his knees begging and praying to God Almighty for a come up. When we step up to fight those enemies, then count me in. I promise that I will battle to the very end and bleed until my veins run dry.

But until then, I refuse to join your ranks and fight for your beliefs and issues while mine are laid by the wayside.

-Marcus A. White

I was working on reading *Black Hawk Down* for the third time when I first started hearing the banging of the war drums. If only President Bush had read it once. If he had, then maybe he would have silenced the pounding of those drums knowing full well that this war would not be a cake walk. Instead it would be a nightmare.

I was standing in the USA Today operations center, watching on the television as videos were sent back from the Middle East of M-1 Abrams tanks and American troops storming across the desert. It was an amazing and historic sight. I remember it like I do the two space shuttles blowing up.

My coworkers were arrogant and cocky regarding the American invasion. I despised their ideas and gung-ho attitudes concerning what we were all witnessing. They seemed to feel as though we were watching the first round of an easy Mike Tyson fight. It was like they were more concerned with seeing how many seconds it would take for Mike to knock the guy out as opposed to how much punishment his opponent could withstand. The guys that I was standing in the room with were all former military. They were each supposed to be a former soldier. That is if you can call a guy that trains to kill and then does four years overseas chasing foreign skirts and getting drunk off of foreign beer, a soldier. I can't. Not after meeting Captain Forseth.

This isn't anything personal against the three guys that I watched the news with that day. I happen to really like one of them. But when it comes to war, I have read and watched as much as I could in order to come to some understanding of what is inside of us that allows us do the things that must be done in one. Those three had none of it and I could listen to their hoorah nonsense no longer. So I asked them a simple question, one that I already knew the answer to.

"You each spent all of that time in the service. You were trained to kill. So now that there is a war going on, if you could, would you go back and fight?"

My logic was simple and used basically to make fun of them. It was probably not a nice thing to do but that operations center turned nice guys into assholes. I knew they all would say no. I knew that because like I said, I read and I have an idea of what real soldiers are like. Plus I now work around true soldiers every day. Old ones that would fight right now if they could. Not because they believe that Sadaam was the devil or even because George Bush told them to. They would fight because they love their country. They are real soldiers that can barely walk, yet always stand for the Pledge of Allegiance. Over sixty years later they still wear their insignias proudly on their hats and jackets and drape the doors of their rooms with American flags. The three guys that I was watching the television with should not even be placed in the same category as the men and women that I talk to every day.

"Why did you three spend all that time training to kill if you are not willing to see if you could actually do it? It is like a spending years in

law school preparing to be an attorney and then graduating without taking the Bar exam or ever trying a real case."

They each agreed that since I never signed up for the military, I didn't understand. But it was them that didn't understand. They didn't understand how it was impossible for me to think like them. And since I was already angry about the start of the war I continued to shoot bullets at the three of them.

"I might not know what it is like to be in the military but I do know that if I was trained to kill I wouldn't rest until I put a bullet in someone's ass…"

I was starting to hit their *"Man"* buttons then. I could feel their anger. They were starting to feel disrespected and it was pissing them off. But unlike the three of them, I can fight for real and considering how I felt about that place, at that time, I would have had no problem tearing that motherfucker up.

My point was to show them that you shouldn't expect people to do something that you aren't willing to do yourself. We were sending kids over there to kill and die and we didn't even really know why. Well I know why but that is another chapter, maybe even another book. Regardless of how far advanced we were militarily, kids were still going to die. It is war and that is what happens in it. I was so angry about the war because I could see clearly that we were being deceived. I just couldn't understand why no one else could. So when I found myself in the midst of warmongers, I kept my guns cocked and close.

I tell people all the time that if I were an Iraqi, I would be an insurgent. Men are supposed to protect their homes, family, children and country. That is what I see them doing over there. There is only one difference that I see between the so-called Iraqi insurgent and the colonists that bravely fought off British rule and oppression to help form this country that I love so much. That difference is oil. If Sadaam didn't have that black gold flooding his backyard like the high waters of Hurricane Katrina, then he wouldn't have had to worry about hiding in that spider hole. I am sure of that.

If I were to wake up tomorrow morning to see my Southeast streets being patrolled by Iranian or Chinese soldiers, I'm not grabbing the remote and turning on the television to see what the deal is. I'm grabbing some heat and looking to clear the streets. And I wouldn't be alone. You think these city streets are mean and violent now? Put a foreign army on patrol of the south side and watch how many burners come out from under all those mattresses in the hood.

Try as I might I just can't make myself hate the Iraqi's. Even though they are killing my brothers and sisters in arms, I just can't believe that they are the *"homicide bombers"* and murderers that we are made to believe they are. I know they kill civilians, chop heads off and disrespect their women but there is war raging within their country. A war that they didn't choose. Plus, there is this little thing called culture. Which means that not everyone thinks, lives, loves, hates, praises or chooses their leaders the same way.

Our President had many tools in his tool box. Unfortunately, he reached in and grabbed the first one that he saw, *"The Sledge Hammer of War."* I know that somewhere inside that tool box was a small pack of eyeglass screwdrivers that had *"Diplomacy"* written on it. Instead of grabbing one of the screwdrivers to handle the job more delicately, we used that war hammer to smash the leadership of Iraq. We chopped Sadaam's head off of the dragon and in an instant the Iraqi people were leaderless. Of course there would be a power vacuum followed by infighting. I don't understand why the Sunni versus Shiite conflicts came as such a surprise to our government. Even I knew that was coming and I only knew a little about Iraq. That being said, when it boils down to it they are all fighting a common enemy now. Us. Yes the Iraqi's fight brutally and they do things that are unimaginable to most of us. But that just tells me that some people need to have a ruthless, fear-infusing dictator as a leader.

It is crazy that in one fail swoop we have helped to unite countries against us while our own hasn't been this divided since The War Between the States. And also I claim not to be an expert on the arts of war and military tactics and I hate when people say, *"I told you so."* Therefore I won't. But know that damn I sure want to.

Our country is in a state of confusion and I blame our government. We are spread too thin because we are fighting too many battles. The War in Iraq. The War on Poverty. The War on Illegal Immigration. The War on Drugs. The War on Terror. The poor forgotten War in Afghanistan. Soldiers are still dying there. Please don't forget that.

We can't win them all. Which ones are we going to lose? Will continuing to fight them all at once make us lose them all together? I hope everyone is praying to their God like I am because the last days look to definitely be upon us.

14

"In the first place we should insist that the immigrant who comes here in good faith becomes an American and assimilates himself to us, he shall be treated on an exact equity with everyone else for it is an outrage to discriminate against any such man because of creed or birthplace or origin. But this is predicated upon the man's becoming an American and nothing but an American. There can be no divided allegiance here. Any man who says he is an American but something else also, isn't an American at all. We have room for but one flag, the American flag ... We have room for but one language here and that is the English language... and we have room for but one sole loyalty and that is a loyalty to the American people."

-Theodore Roosevelt

Illegal Immigration is a topic that I recently realized is very sensitive to me. In my opinion it is an affront and slap in the face of all of us convicts. Illegal Immigration by definition is against the law. The fact that it is debated and politicized makes me ill. How hypocritical our government has become. It has always been off to the Poke when I sold a rock of coke or got caught with a bag of smoke. I walk around with a bad back and two aching feet limping and skimping trying to make ends meet and what do I see when I turn on the TV? Debates on whether credit cards and driver's licenses should be handed over to people that intentionally broke the law. My driver's license was always among the list of first things that were snatched from me when I went afoul of the law.

When I see the police drive on past a day laborer pick-up site, inside I chuckle at the hypocrisy and think about all the cops that jumped out on me and my friends when we were on the corner selling coke. It's just not fair. And please don't get me wrong. I am not a racist even though I have been called a bigot for feeling this way about Illegal Immigration. Being called a bigot makes me laugh when I think about it. I happen to dislike everyone equally and the things that do make me dislike a person reside far beneath the epidermis, believe me. I just think that you should feel proud to be an American. Even though we are going through some rough times right now, I think that you should be honored to live here as I am and fly our flag or none at all. Nowadays, driving down the highway is like flashing back to ninth grade and Mrs. Korcel's World History class. I'm talking about flags from every nation that you can imagine and yet television news reporters in America can't wear American Flag pins on their lapels without someone calling for their head.

Help wanted signs don't stay up long in the hood, so the argument that illegals are doing the work that Americans don't want to do, is false. I see poverty every single day. And I wonder how many of the men on the corner of First and Upsal would be flipping burgers and mowing grass instead of getting drunk and all day sitting on their ass if they had the option of catching the bus to the McDonald's down the street, make a few dollars and sneak some chicken nuggets to eat.

I understand that poorer countries see America as the land of milk and money. I understand why they want to get here and the last thing that I would want to do is stop someone from having a better life or step on their dream. That is not my style. But once again, there is room for the felon's argument. We *(felons)* don't do what we do because we enjoy it. I don't know one drug dealer that does so for any other reason than trying to have a better life. It isn't cool to sell drugs anymore. It used to be attractive, flashy, addictive and dangerous. Now it is just dangerous. But my point is that just like selling those rocks of cocaine; hopping that fence and running across the desert in a desperate attempt for better food, more money and a new life—IS ILLEGAL!!! My friend Lee wanted a better life. He wanted a nicer house. He wanted his children to have a happier childhood than he had. He was willing to break the law to make all that happen. Striving for sweet dreams of better possibilities that were rooted in unlawful ambition, Lee illegally crossed the line and when he was caught he was sent back to prison. But if he had illegally crossed the border, then he might still be here to raise his children, eat good food and watch Redskins games with us. Lee knew the consequences for breaking the law. The rules to The Game are specific. He knew that if he got caught then he was going back to the pen for a long time. Those rules are why he didn't expect street closing, metro filling and traffic congesting rallies to be held in his honor. It was nothing personal. The Game is The Game.

I watched the news clips of the Illegal Immigration rights rallies held all over the country, DC, Chicago, LA. And what stuck out the most to me was that I saw hardly any American Flags. I couldn't believe that I was watching a rally with foreigners demanding rights for illegals in our country and they couldn't even wave our flag. The fact that thousands of people were demanding equal rights for people that broke the law would have been amusing to me if I didn't find it all so offensive. As a convicted felon, I know that equal rights are also on that list of the first things to go when you break the law and if I hadn't spent four years in the pen for doing just that and another thirteen suffering through the aftermath caused by it, then I might feel more sympathetic about Illegal Immigration. But I did and I am, so I don't. You do the crime. You do the time. I did.

15

"I've been to prison. I ain't going back."
-Kiefer Sutherland, Truth or Consequences NM (1997)

My good friend Lee called me not long after he got arrested this last time. I didn't really know what to say to him and was thankful that he only had a few minutes and therefore couldn't talk long. He just wanted me to know that he was okay and that a letter was coming.

About two days after the phone call I received the letter from him. I got home from work, checked the mail and there it was sitting there in the mailbox like a letter from the I.R.S. I didn't want to read it. Actually I didn't read it, at least not immediately. I didn't read it because I was worried about what would be in it. Lee's letter sat on the table for days and I found myself watching it from time to time like it was going to hatch.

Finally, after a couple of days, I got up the nerve to read it and afterwards I wished I hadn't. Understandably, he was really vague about how he got caught and who was involved. I knew that information would require a visit. But he was crystal clear about the way he was going to live his life from now on. That was the part that bothered me.

Lee had been doing time for one reason or another for almost as long as I can remember. He never brushed going to prison off like it wasn't a big deal. But, considering what he was involved in, he never seemed to really fear it like you would think either. Although, it was not a place that he desired to be, he seemed to function better behind bars than anyone I ever knew. It was that fact that lent me a little relief as he started off on his new prison adventure. It was also that fact that threw me for a loop after reading his letter.

I don't know exactly what type of vibe I was expecting to get from him as I waited for his letter. I guess maybe I expected to hear some sadness in his words and a lot of anger in the messy trail left by the lead of his pencil. But what I felt from him when I actually read it was defeat. I was reading the words of a beaten man. He played The Game. He lost. And from his own words I could tell that he realized it.

In my first book I wrote about the *"adjusting"* stage that comes along with doing time. Hope is actually a better word to describe the period of confusion that inmates go through during the initial stage of incarceration. Home is not an option anymore and all that awaits is a number. That number fits into a range and represents how many years you will spend in the shit. Most spend months and sometimes even a year in jail waiting to finally get their sentence. During that time period, basically, you get religion. You pray. You beg and plead. You go to church, read your Bible or Koran and promise your God that if He will get you out of jail and back home you will never commit another crime as long as you live. *Cross my heart.*

To me Lee was a veteran when it came to prison time. I always figured that he could handle whatever sentence he got and bit with the best of them. So when I read his letter and saw that it was filled with talk of turning his life over to God, reading the Bible and going to church; I was almost brought to tears because I knew that if he was talking like that then that meant he was hurting bad. Like the voice at the end of the phone after a wrong number is accidentally dialed in the dark, my lifelong friend Lee sounded like a stranger.

I expected to read the paragraph about how hard it was going to be for him to do time while having small children on the outside. I also expected the paragraph about how I am someone that he considered to be a true friend. I wasn't prepared in the least for all of the lines about his religious conversion. Part of me wants to believe that his change is legit. But my personal prison experience and the criminal still roaming around inside tells me that he is still *"adjusting."*

I wondered to myself, *"How do I respond to this letter?"*

Considering the fact that I am a published author that has been to prison, you would think that jail-letter writing would be easy for me. It is not. It is funny but I always found that type of writing to be extremely difficult. Writing a letter back to Lee after reading his was harder than any jail-letter that I've written previously. I only wanted him to know that I was going to be there for him. But that letter would have only been two lines long and I knew he needed more. So I talked about my book to use as filler and told him that I was going to have my publisher send him a copy.

I also told him that, considering the fact that I know firsthand what he is experiencing, I wasn't sure if his religious *"conversion"* was legitimate or just a phase that he was going through during his period of adjustment. But either or, I had his back and I would do my best to help him and his family. I told him to put me and Poogie on his visiting list and that we were coming to see him even if he landed in Texas.

I was finally able to send his family a little cash. Considering what I owe him, it wasn't much at all. But not long afterwards, I got a call from him thanking me for helping out. He asked me when I could come see him. I could tell from the brief conversation that he had things he wanted to tell me. Like who the fucking rat was, how it all went down, what he expected of me, etc. But that wasn't a conversation that either of us were willing to have on the phone. So I knew that I had to go see him. We locked in the next Wednesday at 7:50P.M.

Going to see Lee in jail was not something I was looking forward to. But I knew it was something I had to do. I got out of prison a couple of years before Lee did the last time. That meant that I got the chance to visit him at each institution that he got transferred to before his release. Those visits were always laid back and funny. We would load the car up and road trip to wherever Lee was kept. Back then Lee was comfortable in his surroundings and most importantly he didn't have any kids on the outside growing up without him. So we would all sit there, drink soda, eat chips, look at other guy's girls, laugh and talk about whatever. We were young, wild and carefree. We felt that we still had some good years left ahead of us. And although growing up none of us wanted to have to actually experience the prison experience, we still felt that if we had to lose a few years, it was better to get the loss out of the way early.

This time was different. This time there were children involved. This time there were bills and houses involved. This time we were too old to afford the loss of time and too needed to throw away months let alone years. Basically, this time was going to hurt. And I mean bad. A prison sentence at our age will affect a lot more than just Mama. A grown-up prison sentence brings along with it a list of collateral damage that is taller, *taller than the Empire State* and the pain caused spreads wider, *wider than Victoria Lake.* It was just too early for a visit, too early after his arrest I mean. I knew that it hadn't sunk in all the way yet for him. I knew that I would be able to see his pain and that is what made me dread going to see him that soon.

Starving, I took the metro a few stops out of the city and into Alexandria. Once I arrived at my stop, I got off and walked the two or three blocks to the jail.

Whoever designed and built the Alexandria jail knew exactly what they were doing. It is a threatening and ominous structure and fortunately it is one jail in the area that I haven't graced with my presence. Well one time I was in their custody but that was only for a few hours. I never made it upstairs, thankfully. As I walked down the sidewalk leading away from the metro stop, I could see the building looming in the distance like a big red fortress. The monstrous building is too tall for the trees to hide its face and it stared at me hungrily. The criminal that is inside of me always hates going willingly to any jail, police station or prison. Because of those feelings I watched the building with cautious eyes as I walked towards it hoping all the time that it would not swallow me whole and soul.

I walked into the entrance where there were two cops waiting. They looked at me the way all cops look at me. Or at least the way I think all cops look at me. I was dreading any questions or conversations from or with them. One of them asked who I was there to see. I gave them Lee's name and held my breath as he looked at the Visiting List. He looked up at me and said sternly and cop-like, *"You are an hour early. You have to come back."* Guess who got there an hour early? Me. Someone who never gets anywhere early. Damn.

I had to kill some time but I was walking so I needed to take travel time into consideration. I decided to go eat. A McDonald's or Wendy's would have been perfect but just my luck there was nothing. I had to basically walk all the way back to the metro, cross the street and look near the movie theaters to find a place to eat. I sat down at a Ruby Tuesday's and for some reason decided to be daring with my order. I say daring because I don't eat a lot of foods. Or combinations of foods. Or foods of certain colors. Or foods of certain textures. Or foods from certain countries. I could go on but I won't. Anyway, I ordered a buffalo burger. Whoa. It has been something that I always wanted to try ever since I watched *Dances with Wolves*. As I waited for my *Tatanka Burger* to be cooked I noticed that time was ticking away. My food wasn't ready and I still had to walk back to the jail. Finally I decided that I would have to come back. I paid for my food and told the waitress that I would be back to get it before they closed.

I speed-walked back to the jail. This time instead of taking the sidewalk, I cut across an open field that separated the jail and metro station. It was dark and the grass crumbled beneath my feet as I maneuvered my way, by moonlight, down the slight path left by others that previously made the same trek as I.

This time there were no officers waiting for me at the entrance. That concerned me. I know from experience that visiting hours are very strict. I was almost ten minutes late and was worried that I came all the way out there for nothing. I followed the signs pointing in the direction of the visiting area. As I got to the end of it I could see a hallway crowded with about twenty people. It was the next group of visitors. They were early for their visits while the clock was already quickly ticking away on mine. I rang the gate and received a tongue lashing from the lady guard on duty for being late. I took her shit. But only because she was cute. She buzzed me in and had me walk through the metal detector. As always I set the damn thing off. Sometimes I think I have a metal fragment embedded in my body somewhere.

I was told to take the elevator upstairs. I got on the elevator with a straight up *"Fly Girl,"* she was made up all pretty and was late like me. I could tell from the way she smiled at me that whoever her man was, he was in trouble. I hoped he didn't have a lot of time to do because she was not going to keep it real with him if he was away for more than a minute.

We stepped off of the elevator into a room with lots of women seated at small booths with telephones inside of them. All of the women looked through dirty windows the size of a bathroom mirror into the faces of their man, son or brother. The *"Fly Girl's"* man came out almost immediately. He tried not to look pressed but I could tell he was. Lee made me wait. I heard them call his name but it still seemed like forever before he came out.

Back in the day, sitting down at a table with a group of friends and cousins to wait for Lee to come out to join us was an easier experience than what I experienced the other day. The last time I had to visit Lee in prison we were counting down the days until his release and talking about what he was going to do when he got home. This time was going to be a different scene completely.

The visiting area was separated in half. I didn't know which side Lee was going to come out on so I just stood alone in the middle of the room so I could see both doors. The door opened on my right but thankfully it wasn't Lee. The right side of the room was really packed and I hate to feel crowded. A few minutes later Lee emerged from the back door of the left side of the visiting room and picked up the phone.

I walked over to the booth. He didn't look like he was missing out on any meals and it looked like he added a few tattoos since the last time I saw him in a wife-beater. There was a stool there in the booth but I didn't sit down and neither did he. I picked up the phone and said, *"Man, I hoped we were done with this shit."* He agreed and we both shook our heads and breathed a sick sigh of recognition. I sure was right about one thing, though. I could definitely see his pain.

He reaffirmed to me his new religious conversion. He didn't go too deep into how the whole process of finding God came about and I didn't ask any questions. I just let him talk. Honestly, I didn't think he felt comfortable talking to me about it. I know that some things easier to write and feel than to say so I didn't mind avoiding that particular subject. And after all, he was the one on lock. He had to stay there and do whatever it took to deal, while all I had to do was hop a train and go home.

I realized during my visit with Lee that I was more comfortable when I was on the other side of the glass. I mean the *"inside-side."* I wonder why that is. Standing there with only an inch of glass separating me from incarceration, I felt totally apprehensive. I felt shaky and the need to keep the conversation moving but I didn't know what to say. He told me who the snitch was and just like I figured it was someone close. A no-count that we let roll and shoot ball with us. A backstabbing traitor that I hope gets what he has got coming. It infuriates me because that just makes doing the time that much harder for Lee. As if he didn't already have enough stresses on his mind with his kids, his girl and the house now he has to do his time knowing that someone close to him helped snatch his ass off of the streets.

Since he was a three time loser, Lee decided to take a plea instead of going in front of a jury and risking a life sentence. Ordinarily Lee would have had his sentence and been shipped out of state by now. But his lawyer is postponing the sentencing date while the laws affecting crack cocaine offenses are reviewed. It seems that someone somewhere is finally coming to his senses. I never understood how you could get more time for selling crack than you would if you got caught selling powder coke of the same weight. Better late than never I guess.

When our time was up, we gave each other a pound through the glass. I secretly wished him good luck and watched as he turned and walked through the door. As I headed back to the elevator I selfishly thanked God that it wasn't me headed back into that cage.

The one place I can actually see my growth as a man is in my forethought. When I was younger, my concerns never made it past the jail cell. Now that I am older, I think of how my actions would affect my children, my family, friends and even coworkers. All I could think about as I walked out of that jail was, *"Damn, what if Stan and Marjie had to come see me here? The shame. Game over for me. No more signs needed God. I hear you."*

16

"Learn from the lessons that the job has to offer."
-Miss Kay Jiles

So many of us work a job that we hate. And as bad as the job can be, most are completely willing to retire from that job at 55 or whatever age requirement and begin the journey of happiness. *"When I retire I am going to move to Florida." "When I retire I am going to travel the world."* I don't think like that. I refuse to do something I hate for twenty or thirty years before finally getting around to doing something I love. How many people work a crummy job for thirty years and then drop dead two weeks into retirement? Too many and believe me when I say that you will not add my name to that bucket list.

Fortunately I don't work a job that I hate. I work a job that I love and because of that I have time to plan. I tell people all the time that I am on a *"One Year Plan."* That doesn't mean that in one year I am going to quit my job and become totally self-sufficient. What it means is that if I do what I am supposed to do during the next year and my cards fall right, then work should be an option or in my case a luxury.

I briefly mentioned my job earlier when I talked about my memories of the First Annual Poetry on the Greene Festival but my poem and sentences didn't do *The Soldier's Home* total justice. I have been thinking really hard about this chapter and it has been tough because I just can't put my finger on what it is about my job that makes me love it so much. Is it the old soldiers? Is it the staff? Is it the place? Is it the history? Is it the commute? I just don't know. I had lunch with Miss Kay one day and she told me why she loved working there. It was an enlightening experience but lunch with Miss Kay always is.

She is a woman full of knowledge, compassion, love and opinions. She is what I would hope to be like if I get to be her age. She is more than just grandmotherly, she's definitely that but she seems so well versed and in tune with life that I just have to listen when she talks.

I said to her in between bites of my cheeseburger, *"Miss Kay, how do you feel about working here at the home? Do you like it? A lot of people don't seem happy and I can't understand it because I love it here."*

She placed her fork down on the table and sat back in her chair like she was full but she had barely started eating before I asked her my question so I knew she was about to hit me with some religion. Miss Kay is very religious and very passionate about her relationship with God but at the same time very *"common sensible"* about it. That is why I feel comfortable talking with her about anything. There is no judging with her. She looked at me like I was crazy and said, *"Oh yes. What better place could you be?"*

Her voice went quiet and then she breathed a heavy sigh. Her head went back and she stared at the cafeteria's ceiling like she was looking up at the midnight sky searching for shooting stars. When she brought her head back down to face me, she pulled off her glasses and I could see that she was crying. She dabbed at her eyes with a napkin, looked at me and said, *"What a blessing from God it is to be able to spend the last moments of life on earth with these men and women. We are the last people they see before they see God. How beautiful is that?"*

What could I say to that? I love Miss Kay.

I know the old soldiers are dying and they know it too so I felt a little funny mentioning that *"his time was not long"* in my poem that I read back at the poetry festival. I hate watching them near the end of their roads and if there is a downside to working at the home it is the *Final Retreat* board. The *Final Retreat Board* is a glass enclosed case that is filled with names and photos of the recently deceased and it is there that I find out why I haven't seen some of my old friends in a few days and why I won't ever see them again. I notice when there is a new posting even before I get close enough to actually see the face. I always hope that, one; it isn't one of the guys that I know well and two; that it isn't a lady. I hate seeing the pictures of the ladies. They disturb me.

I was standing in front of the Final Retreat board one morning when I noticed that Mrs. Hampton died. She came to the home from Gulfport, Mississippi after Hurricane Katrina left her and a few hundred other old vets homeless. I could tell that she was not happy living in Washington and missed Gulfport greatly. I overheard her talking one day about her former home in Mississippi. She had a view of the gulf and at night could see the lights of the shrimp boats off in the distance. She said it was beautiful. She dressed in pretty pink outfits and always looked like she was going somewhere. I passed her in the halls and said hello many times but she never returned any of my greetings. I always wondered why she seemed so angry. Maybe it was because she didn't want to be this close to *"up north."* She did seem like an old *Southern Bell*. Maybe she missed her husband. He did die only days after they were married. Maybe she knew she was close to the end. I'd bet it was the latter.

Getting old does something to all of us. I feel it in my knees, see it in the gray hairs that stick out of my face and I am constantly aware of its presence during my drive to success. Models can fight back the aging process with face lifts and implants. Athletes can ward it off with steroids and human growth hormones. But for old soldiers, there is nothing. And if getting old takes something from the rest of us, it really deals a mighty blow to soldiers.

From my limited experience I believe that in order to be a good soldier you must first have some Type-A personality traits. Meaning that you must be proud, hard-working, self-motivated, driven, multi-functional, impatient and independent. Those are not traits that you grow out of. I know that because I have seen an old soldier spend the night on the floor, wallowing in his own urine and feces, after falling on his way to the bathroom. Unable to get up, all he had to do was knock the phone off the hook and help would have come running. But because he was very proud and on top of that, stormed the beaches of Normandy, there was no way he would have a pretty nurse come in and see him in that condition. So he just lay there. All night long. I wonder what he thought about. I wonder if he cried.

I read about this cat that lived in a nursing home. Whenever someone was about to die the cat would crawl up into the bed with the person. The very next morning the person would be dead. Not in a couple of weeks. Not in a couple of days. I mean the very next day. Sometimes within hours. I don't quite have that same ability but I can tell when the end is not far for one of the home's residents. They have a look about them that spills the beans and it happens almost overnight. One day I will see a resident standing in line for lunch, chatting with his friends with a smile on his face. The next day or so I will see him watching television all by himself down at the hospital building. Gone is the smile. Gone is the color. Gone is the light. He will perk up when he sees me and try to carry on a conversation like everything is normal but we both know what time it is. I can tell by the grayness of his face that his old ticker isn't keeping good time anymore.

If I have learned anything from being around these old soldiers, it is to respect my youth, my health and my elders. And also to not wait to tell someone how you feel about them. I was talking to an old soldier in the days before he died and I remember that he seemed to feel sorry. I don't know what exactly he was sorry about, as it could be any number of things when you have lived that long but he was definitely bothered about something. I chose not to pry because if these residents want to tell you something, they will. You don't have to pull anything out of them. So after I left him I sat at the front desk and watched him watch television. All I could think was, *"I don't want to die alone."*

I've only worked at the home for two years so getting used to watching the old soldiers die so frequently is still a process that I am not all the way comfortable with. I am happy that the face on the *Final Retreat* board is an old face and that the person obviously led a long life with lots of grandchildren and family memories. But it is still death and unlike Miss Kay, to me, spending the last moments of life with someone is only creepy. And to add to the discomfort that I feel, it is hard saying goodbye to someone every time you see them and know that it is a very good chance that it is the *"Long Goodbye."* I work at a retirement home where death is always just a day away for a lot of people that I care about. I have lost a lot of old soldier friends but only one that I really considered a true one. I don't find myself worrying about the deaths of too many residents as by the time their end comes they are usually widows or widowers but I do worry about the Logan's. Selfishly, I worry that the death of either of them is going to cause a Domino Effect and take out the other one immediately after, causing me to lose two good friends basically at once.

I met the Logan's in the cafeteria during lunch one day. She noticed my book that I had on my tray for some reason. She asked me what it was about. I was a little nervous admitting to a little old lady that I used to be locked up. But I did and she replied, *"My husband and I used to work in a prison ministry at Lorton when we were younger. Bring a copy of your book by my room. I want to get one from you."* Since then she has bought more copies of my book than anyone else. She sends them to her children. She sends them to her friends. She is proud of me and the changes I have made in my life.

Mr. Logan is the legs and Mrs. Logan is the ears. She can hardly walk and he can barely hear so they need each other. When they first came to the home the idea was floated to them that they might have to be separated. What did they say that for? Mrs. Logan completely lost it. *"We have been together for 65 years! He's the legs and I'm the ears. We can't be separated!"* Her screams and cries echoed throughout the Wellness Center. Needless to say they were not separated and now I get to watch in amazement as the two of them act as one. It is like they are one soul. One body. One mind. That unification is what concerns me. I worry that each one is keeping the other alive so, like I said before, when I lose one I lose two. I see them together so much that when I see them apart it looks strange to me. I want the Logan's to live forever. I check on them from time to time because I know they are leaving soon. They know it too but what's funny is when they talk to me they don't make me feel like they are dreading anything. Because of their strong relationship with God they seem to live freely, stress-free and content with their only real concern being for the other. I am impressed with their seeming ability to fight back and yet face Death head-on as long as they can do it together. That is real love.

The Logan's are old and dying but like I said, I don't think about it when I am talking to them. They make me think about long life and togetherness. But I can't say that for all of the old soldiers. All I can think about with some residents is death. Some have made me feel like they felt bad for me because they were dying. Like their death was a burden on me. Crazy I know. On the flip side some have made me feel like I was responsible for them dying. Not literally but they were just so mad that their time was almost up that they just hated everybody. Roy could give off that impression from time to time. He was that one true friend that I was talking about.

To people that didn't know him Roy Pickel was a grumpy old man. Those of us that took the time to fight past the outer shell know that he was charming, friendly and fun to be around. Anyone that really knows me also knows that I am a war history buff. What better place to work could there be for me? I love reading books and watching movies based on wars from the past to the present but to actually hear about the Band of Brothers from one of the actual brothers is something that is just skin tingling to me. It was destined for me to work at that home I know it. *(Honestly, I don't even remember applying for the job. I just got the call one day and the rest is history.)*

Roy Pickel was a *"Toccoa Man,"* meaning that he was an original member of Easy Company, 506 Parachute Infantry Regiment of the 101st Airborne Division, United States Army. When I found out who he was I made it a point to get to know him. Talking to him for the first time I felt like I was in the presence of royalty.

I said to him, *"Mr. Pickel, it is an honor to meet you, sir."*

Naturally he griped at me and said, *"Do you see my damn hat? What does it say?"*

He always wore a white and blue baseball cap that said, *"My Name is Roy"* in big blue letters. I don't know how I could have missed that. I think I was too star struck or something.

"I'm sorry. It is an honor to meet you Roy. I have read all about what you guys went through back during the war and I am proud that I can tell people that I met you."

"Hell, I didn't do nothing." Was his response.

He didn't do nothing? That is the response from a lot of soldiers that have faced the horrors that world war brings with it and made it back home to talk and write about it. They don't want the fame, glory and praise heaped on them. They want it placed on the men that didn't make it back. The men that died for them. With the men that gave their all so their buddies could live is where the honor belongs if you ask an old soldier (or a young one nowadays.) But that doesn't mean that just because you survived the war that you are not a hero. No way could it ever mean that to me.

I spent a lot of time with Roy before he died. He was moved from his own room down to the hospital building and absolutely hated it. He thought he was fine but I'm not a doctor and I saw his feet one time and fine was one of the things that he was not. Even I knew that. His feet looked like they were about to pop. They were so swollen that I know his shoes had to be three or four sizes too big and even then they were still tight. I am sure he was in excruciating pain every single day. *(I know foot pain.)* Just like a lot of old soldiers that have to make the trip *"down the hill"* to the hospital building, Roy fussed and fussed to get out of there and back up on the hill to his own room. But unlike a lot of old soldiers that made that trek *"down the hill,"* Roy actually came back. He won his battle and I was not shocked when I saw him motoring his BPV down the hall with the throttle wide open. If I had known that he would be dead in a matter of days I would have made a quicker effort to see him. But of course I didn't and now the sight of his back, as he sped down the hall in his motorized wheelchair, is the last memory I have of actually seeing a great man alive.

Roy was cremated and his remains were buried at Arlington National Cemetery. I have had a lot of my old soldier friends die since I have been working at the home. Roy was the only one whose funeral I attended. I hate funerals and find myself always vowing not to attend anymore but once again I found myself feeling compelled to enter a place with people dressed in dark clothes and speaking in quiet voices.

I have never heard anyone speak of Pastor John Goodloe with anything other than a great deal of respect, admiration and appreciation. And it is well deserved. He is a good man and someone to aspire to be like. The first time I saw him I thought to myself, *"Damn, I bet he had a mean low post game when he was younger, probably still does."* He is fifty-five, about 6'4" and around 250 pounds so physically he is towering and imposing.

And even more impressive than his NBA-sized frame, is his heart that seems to be the size of Paul Bunyan's. And please don't let me forget about his voice. It is a mesmerizing oratory mixture of the deep reverberations of James Earl Jones and the smooth eloquence of Barak Obama. You just have to listen to him because his voice makes you stay still.

I have heard him lead a prayer before and I have talked to him often throughout the time that I have worked at the home but I had never actually seen him in his *"element."*

It wasn't until Roy's funeral that I first got the chance to see him *"shine."*

Before the service began the family and friends of Roy gathered in a small dimly lit greeting room. Roy was cremated so, fortunately, there was no casket there for me to stare at. I came in alone and immediately introduced myself as a friend of Roy's from the retirement home. His son was there and greeted me very kindly. Pastor Goodloe came in and circled the room offering words of kindness and remorse to Roy's family members and friends. I thought to myself as I watched him do his thing, *"Some people are just cut out for the job they do."*

Roy's funeral was not a sad experience. In fact, I didn't see one tear. Funerals for the elderly are not as devastating a process for me as the funerals caused by premature death have always been. So as I stood there at Roy's gravesite, strangely I felt nothing but happiness for him. I felt totally relaxed and stress-free. I didn't even flinch at the sound of the twenty-one gun salute. *(Now that could possibly be from living through four 4th of July holidays in the hood, I don't know.)*

In the end Roy represented the down side to getting old. He had become weak and brittle. Neal on the other hand represents something else. He is a resident at the home as well but he is fighting old age with a passion and seems to be kicking it dead in the ass. I'm ashamed to say so but at his age he is more physically fit than I am. He first introduced himself to me after I read my poem at the Poetry on the Greene Festival. We talked for a few minutes and I told him that the poem was just something I did for the festival, that I prefer writing books. He ended up getting one of my books from me and from there a friendship was born.

Neal bumped into me in the library the other day and told me that he had been trying to catch up with me to talk about my book. He said he had hoped to become my Forrester. My mentor in a way. He felt that he could help me dig deeper into myself and become a better writer.

Just like Sean Connery, my friend Neal is a gray-haired recluse of a man. And he is also very complex. I always see him by himself. He says that he spends so much time alone because he feels there is no one at the home that he can share his knowledge with. He has read my first book one and a half times in an effort to understand me. Not just my surface, as he feels the world is too superficial, he wants to understand the writer in me and how I am able to express my pain so well in my writing.

He said that from reading my book he could tell when I was on my game and writing about something that I was passionate about. He said that he could also tell when I lost focus and my writing seemed to just be filler. I have thought about him a lot as I have been working on this new book and I think that his comments on my first one are what have made writing this book take so long. That is because there is no filler this time. No preservatives either. Every sentence matters.

17

> *"You write the first draft with your heart and the second draft with your head."*
>
> —Sean Connery, *Finding Forrester (2000)*

I pluck moments of history out of my past and piece them together in puzzled paragraphs. Did my writing ability prosper and grow? There are times when I think so but how do I really know? Sure I'd love to win The Pulitzer Prize, to sit there on my mantle right beside my prison basketball MVP, a card from my mama and a snapshot of my kids and a few other reminders of the life I have lived. Approval is motivation and that's a good thing for me as I believe every single keystroke fulfills my destiny. My ghost stories never needed a ghost writer I know that statement as fact. I write my own pain and I'm offended you asked because there's no need to question that. My editor looks for spelling errors and a comma that's out of place. She's a white chick in San Francisco, how could she rewrite the horrors I've faced? She didn't and she doesn't know just what it takes to make my sentences flow. Only I know that. The things that make me tick. And when others question my writing skills it tends to make me sick. Not sick enough to grab my gun but ill enough to make me run. At least the step away that it takes to not feel a hater's breath on my face. Love me or leave me and I love being alone. And when I make it and I will, don't bother picking up the phone. When I write I am at peace. When I write I am taken away. Sometimes to a place I don't want to be, sometimes just a pretty day. Some filled with beautiful flowers and trees and others with clouds and rain. Writing gives me separation and I need it to ease my pain.

The Tree and Me

A touch of autumn fills me with thoughts of the orange and brown leaves the new season has brought. And tall trees once green now yellow and gold, filled to the leaf-stem with stories to be told. Can you imagine all of the history that could be found in the bark of a great oak tree? Born from an acorn during the times of slavery, it grew up through an era of ignorance but survived its misery. Its rings are riddled with bullets from the War Between the States. Its limbs are scarred by nooses from where black men met their fates. Its adolescent trunk was used as cover for a soldier and his gun. And as a place to hide and rest behind for a free slave that was on the run. It nervously watched through leaf-covered eyes as men took wing and soared about the sky. Up over its treetops like birds in the night went those two crazy white guys whose last name was Wright.

And then there are the ten thin oak trees planted on a grassy knoll. They were waiting for Mr. Kennedy and the events of the day to unfold. When the shots rang out, the ten trees began to shout, "There the shooter goes!" But nobody could understand their screams so now nobody knows. The history books say it was Oswald and that is what most will believe. But the real answers are sealed deep down in the roots of that group of ten oak trees.

Man, if I could only see the things that I could have if I were a tree. What a great pleasure I'm sure life would be. The breeze, the stars, the imagery. It has seen it all and still stands tall and every November when its leaves begin to fall, I thank God for the existence of the tree and the tree thanks God that it's not me.

I'm a troubled soul and far from free and that's why the tree would hate to be me. I want to be a better father. I want to raise perfect kids. I want to do lots of good things now to even out all the bad that I did. But it's hard. Really hard. And when bills start to stack up and unknown callers keep calling it's hard to keep my house of cards from burning, crashing or falling. But two faces too cute come flying to my rescue just when things are the bleakest. They're faster than a speeding bullet and more powerful than a locomotive and they catch me when I'm at my weakest.

My two little girls are my crime fighters now. They're my Batman and Robin when The Joker is in town. My two superheroes that keep me straight and they do it with love and no masks on their face. The Joker, he's my nemesis. He's drugs, he's bills and he's fines. He's everything that makes me think of leading a life of crime. But when I think about my kids, I see rainbows and cloud-filled skies. Instead of prison bars and police cars and other things that made my mother cry. My kids they're my life and they matter more than air. If it were not for the two of them my life I'd live without care. I struggle everyday to make their load lighter but if my efforts are not rewarded with gold. Then I hope they one day can read my written words and take pride in the stories I have told.

I think this chapter sounded better before I edited it. But it was kind of messy and I think only rappers would have understood it. But for once, I followed the rules and just wrote from my heart. I have to say, it was a challenge to write this chapter but not as hard as I thought it would be. I am still looking for the writer inside of me and am still trying to figure out what I can do versus what I cannot.

But I honestly wish I could write a whole book that rhymed. That would be some feat and is something to think about for the future. But for now I will just stick to writing like I do and leave the rhyming to the rappers.

18

> *"When you don't use your words correctly or wisely, the result is catastrophic."*
>
> *-KRS-1*

Bill Cosby was bashed and lambasted for saying that our dirty laundry gets out of school everyday at 3:30PM. I ride the Green Line of the Metro and even though it is usually after 4:30PM that I get onboard, I still very much agree with the assessment of the great Mr. Cosby. I made a promise to myself that I am intervening the next time I hear a foul-mouthed fourteen-year-old girl loudly tell the whole train about how she was about to slap the shit out of the fucking bitch that looked at her funny in the cafeteria that morning. Enough is enough. When did it become cool and cute for little girls to cuss like sailors? I remember when I was a teenager; I fought and got kicked out of school. I cussed, drank beer and wine, sold drugs and smoked weed. I did a lot of things that I shouldn't have. But even on my most criminally-minded day, I still showed respect when adults were present, especially older ladies. And when I did my dirt I didn't do it proudly. All you have to do nowadays is sit quietly on a metro bus and listen to all types of criminal confessions. As I sit and listen to these youngin's spill all their business to any ear in range it makes me wonder, *"What could possibly be in store for them?"*

And also, I wore clothes that fit. The young girls wear jeans that are too small and their bellies squeeze and pour out the top and hang below their too tight shirts. And their cracks are always displayed prominently like showing people your ass is a new fashion statement. Don't get me wrong. I love a big old juicy butt. But at least ask me my name before you show it to me. One time I was behind this young girl and all of her meat was tucked so tightly into her jeans that I could not tell if it was her back hanging out or the top of her ass. I say cover it all up.

The young boys are just the opposite. They wear jeans that are too big, sometimes more than two sizes too big and they hang off their asses like my prison jumpsuit used to. I watched a young boy crossing the street one day and he had to stop twice to pull his pants up. I was like, *"How could he possibly think he looks cool?"* I was young once and understand wanting to be down with the latest styles. But all styles aren't good styles, every look isn't always the right one and honestly sometimes I am embarrassed when I see the way white people look at a group of loud and rude black teenagers. Why not take pride in your appearance first as the absolute very least you can do to reach for success? And from a gesture as simple as pulling your damn pants up you might then learn to take some pride in yourself. And then who knows? Maybe you might step up to the next level and be ready to take pride in your work and maybe even one day your children.

Damn, my man Sean Taylor just died. What in the world is going on?

I can clearly see the effects everyday but what are the causes of this behavior in our children? I'm no pediatric psychologist so I don't have any case studies to base my opinions on other than life experience, bus and metro train rides. I don't know anything for sure but since this is my book I am going to voice my opinions and print them as though they are fact.

I blame Dad first. I blame his ass because from birth, whether he has a son or daughter, he should be the trendsetter. He should be the pacemaker that keeps the heart pumping smoothly and the one who provides the spark when things go off track. *(And they will.)* I talked about irresponsible fathers in my first book and as a writer I try not to be redundant but this is a topic that I am very sensitive about. Addressing this problem and then fixing it can solve so many troubles and save so many lives. But just like most of the problems that affect black communities, not having a father in the lives of their children doesn't get mentioned until the kid gets to jail. That is when lawyers, jailors, judges and other people that don't really care decide to pry into his family life looking for the roots and causes of the youngster's criminal behavior. I don't know if I would have skipped prison if my father had been in my life. Sometimes I believe that it was destined for me to go. But I do believe that my chances of going would have at least been greatly reduced by his presence in my life. I am sure that I would have rebelled a bit but maybe, just maybe, if I had a Dad that I looked up to and was proud of, then possibly I would have feared tarnishing his name or worse than that, leaving some of my ass skin on his belt. But I didn't and neither do a lot of these young killers out here roaming my Southeast streets. So Dad, once again, from me and all the young fatherless brothers running wildly around the hood--Fuck you.

Next is Mom. *(Not my mom, of course.)* I'm talking about the moms that either directly or indirectly, teach their daughters that getting knocked up and waiting on a child support check is an acceptable means of making a living.

Social Services and Child Welfare in this country should be called Mother Protection Services because it is a completely one-sided organization and targets fathers unjustly and indiscriminately. I don't believe that child support should be abolished, that would be ridiculous. I just believe that the courts should investigate cases thoroughly and get the whole picture instead of immediately taking up sides with the mothers. I don't believe that all fathers should be lumped into the *"Bad Dad"* category and threatened with wage garnishments and accompanied visits just because things didn't work out with the mother or because she can't pay her own bills. This next statement might come as a shock to some of you but when I found out the motive behind the D.C. Sniper shootings could possibly be related to the custody of his children, I stepped out of myself for a minute. I found that I understood where John Allen Muhammad's rage was coming from and that on a lesser level, I could relate. He lost a bitter custody battle and felt that Child Protection Services painted him a villain long before he became one. He loved his children, wanted them back and was obviously willing to do whatever it took to do so. Even if that meant killing many others to provide cover for killing his wife. I am not saying that loving his kids justified that murderous rampage. I am just speaking personally and testifying that when I lost mine, realized that I had to share them with other men and then that my paycheck was going to be garnished for child support; I wanted to kill my children's mother.

Our child support case came not long after I found out that Chrisi had the kids not telling me about her 800 pound gorilla in the corner. I had been out of the house for over four years by then and had always made sure that Chrisi had money even when I knew that giving her cash would leave me with none. I did this because I felt that even though I was not living there anymore and that was mostly my fault, they were still my responsibility. They, meaning Chrisi as well as the kids. Therefore she always got her money and for a while even got twice what I would have been required to give. But when I found out that the Jake was waking up around my kids, sitting his dirty ass on the same toilet seat that my babies have to use and washing his black ass in the same tub that Deja and Desiree bathe in, basically

I said, *"Fuck you Chrisi. It's only about the kids now. You will not have two niggas taking care of your ass. At least not if you expect me to be one of them."*

The next thing I know I am getting served with Child Support papers by a large black man that banged on my door like he was the police. I sat down and looked over the paperwork and got angrier with every sentence. I was looking at words like *"wage garnishment"* and forgive me but being labeled the *"non-custodial"* parent just seemed to lessen something in me. I know it only means that the kids don't live with me. But for some reason the term typed out with my name next to it took something from me. I was already doing more than what the Court was trying to force me to do and had been doing so for years but to hold a piece of paper in my hand *"ordering"* me to take care of my kids simply embarrassed and infuriated me. It was like Chrisi went to Social Services with a grocery list of what she wanted and like a genie squeezing her fat ass out of a bottle; they granted her every wish without even contacting me to let me know that all of my business was in the street.

I appealed the ruling immediately. Not because I didn't want to take care of my children. I appealed it because I was already taking care of my children and was not going to let a panel full of hens control my money. Naturally, Social Services immediately contacted Chrisi to inform her of my appeal. They probably did it with a nice letter or phone call, while they sent Kimbo Slice to inform me of what was going on. Not fair. My only issue, other than the fact that I was being ordered to pay in the first place, was with the wage garnishment. But those Social Services bitches told her that I appealed because I didn't want to pay the amount. That was a total lie. One that I believe was made up just to keep shit going. At that time things between Chrisi and I were as bad as could be but I was slowly starting to simmer my anger down. That lie perpetuated the drama that Chrisi and I were going through and I know that it was intentionally used by Social Services to cause more separation on our end.

By the time my court date came around, Chrisi and I had worked out our issues, at least the financial ones. And when I told Social Services that we were dropping the case they called me a liar in every word except that one and rushed to get Chrisi on the phone. In the meantime, I was told that if I my story was incorrect my payments will start the first of next month. I was like, *"Start? What do you mean start? They never stopped."*

The hen on the other end of the phone was like, *"Well, Mr. White you were not obligated to make any payments until after the Court's final decision."*

Social Services? Child Protection Services? What kind of service or child protection is involved when the father can legally go two months without paying for the care of his children? I told that bitch, *"Ma'am, I don't know what kind of people you are used to dealing with but I take care of my children. And the fact that I have to sit here and go through this with you and your associates makes me sick."*

Before I could really let the chicken have it, Chrisi was on the phone. They asked her if what I was saying was true and when she said that she wanted the case dropped as well they proceeded to close it but not after letting Chrisi know that she could haul me back in there if need be. It was like they would be waiting for me or something. I felt the threat. I heard it but I moved on. I thanked Chrisi before she hung up and felt a wound begin to heal.

I registered myself on this message board in the area recently in an attempt to market my first book. As soon as I signed on I saw a message thread started named *"Okay my brothers. Where is my child support check?"* Anyone who knows me knows that I had to reply.

The Internet allows you to speak very personally without literally doing it personally so I had to mentally create a face for this chick because I needed to direct my anger and disgust at a person not just a message board. I decided to paint her face a deep smooth ebony after reading that she was tired of hearing sisters cry that they couldn't get their child support checks and her gas tank was low and there were no minutes on her prepaid cell phone. When she said that she didn't want to have to tell her landlord that she didn't get her child support check so she couldn't pay her rent, I decided to put some extensions in her hair and a pair of too tight jeans on a big fat ass. In the minute that it took me to read the posting she put on the message board I had begun to hate her. Her 200 words of finger pointing and blame laying were, in my mind, 200 pieces of shit. And it brought back buried feelings of anger in me that where nothing short of murderous before they were put to rest.

I'm still growing and I see it because my first instinct was to post a reply on the message board blasting that chick out of her shoes. But instead I thought about it and just hit her back with some low key and even tempered common sense. I said to her, *"Why spend your life waiting on a check? Why not teach your children to depend on themselves?"*

In the days before the crack epidemic of the 80's, good mothers were almost a given. Since then a lot of slipping has occurred and that chick's posting on the message board confirmed it for me. It cemented my belief that Mama isn't Mama anymore. I heard a saying once, that said that if you want to see what the mother does all day, watch the daughter. I don't blame Mama for the wildness of our sons. Try as they might and succeed when they can, women are just not meant to teach a boy to become a man. But our daughters, our baby girls are where their hands are needed. I believe that one of the shiny gold keys dangling from the big *"Keychain of Answers"* has *"Little Girls"* engraved on it. And I am not saying that because I have two of them. I just believe that turning things around for us starts with our women, which really means our daughters. If we raise our little girls to view the current behaviors of today's boys and young men as crude and inappropriate then the boys and young men will change. Believe me. Nothing can change a male's opinion of his appearance and attitude faster than the rejection of a female. But instead of telling the slouching long haired boy standing in front of her to stand up straight, cut his hair and pull his pants up, little girls nowadays simply smile and think he is so cute. The next thing you know, she is pregnant and dropping out of school, working a crummy job and on a message board complaining about not getting her child support check. I am sorry but that one is on Mama. Our daughters need to be taught to want better and strive for more. They shouldn't be taught that success in life is simply getting knocked up by a man with money and then hold child support over his head. Not all men with money are good men therefore our little girls need to be taught to choose carefully who they give their love and bodies to. They need to be taught to get what they want in life without some man having to come running to the rescue when things go bad. I encourage my children to draw and write and play sports and just express their creative side. The *"Daily Grind"* is boring and most times unsatisfying so I want them to not have any fear of stepping off the path if that is what will make them happy. Although I want them to be self-reliant, I also want them to know that if they ever really need a man, then I'm their guy. *Boys Beware.*

After Mom and Dad the list goes on from rap, music videos, schools, the media and food. I feel like a hypocrite when I say that rap music perpetuates the problems we now see in our children. I feel like a hypocrite because if there was a soundtrack to the history of my life it would be dominated by rap music. But a different kind of rap. Back during the time when the music seemed to speak to me. It was the kind of music that made me want to dance, jump around or at least bob my head. But most of all I could see talent. The money wasn't nearly as big as it is now so you could feel the love of the music from the artists. You could tell that thought was put into lyrics. So much music nowadays seems to be either tasteless or *talent-less.* And I feel like an old man saying this but its sounds are corrupting our children.

When I was a teen the average dream of other boys my age were to be NBA or NFL stars. It was not a very realistic dream for most of us and one that was easy to outgrow. This new phenomenon of becoming the next big rapper is a different animal it seems. Being a struggling artist myself I can understand, to a degree, the rap affect on our children. Nowadays a hot 16 bars can turn a broke ass hood nigga into a million dollar rap star. And honestly speaking a broke ass hood nigga banging out hooks is no different than a broke ass hood nigga banging out books, all we want is for America to stand up and take a look. Only a brief one and see what we see and how we see it. That the tree of life is filled with nooses of strife and we didn't have to ride a bus to Jena to realize it. The desperate hopes of silver and gold cause these young boys to forget about jobs, degrees and preparing themselves for adult life. That is where I see a difference between them and me. When my book was published I didn't quit my job. I didn't put all of my eggs in one basket and see my name on the cover and think that I was finished. I am never going to step on anyone's dream and I am hoping that isn't how I am coming across. I just hate it when people don't go about striving for their dreams realistically. If you want to be a million dollar rapper then young brother, by all means, go get it. But go get it after school or work. Or before school or work. Or on your lunch break. Or when you get home from school or work. Just not instead of school or work. But that is the case for so many. And in order to pay for rent, food and studio time they do dirt. The dirt leads to jail. Jail leads to a lot more time to rap. More time to rap leads to more thoughts of becoming 50-Cent. More thoughts of becoming 50-Cent lead to less thoughts of getting a job or going back to school when they get out. Not getting a job or going back to school when they get out leads to doing dirt in order to pay for rent, food and studio time. The dirt leads to… Get it?

I just feel that if you are someone that is listened to and you are paid millions of dollars for having people listen to you. Then you have an obligation to your listeners to entertain with some consideration in mind. And if the bulk of your fan base is millions of impressionable children then you really have an obligation. I think if the struggle to become a superstar rapper was rapped about as clearly as the bling and success then maybe the kids of today would understand the risks better. Teenagers buy clothes because rappers tell them to. Kids want certain cars because certain rappers drive them. That being said, to me it isn't out of the realm of possibility that if a successful rapper spoke out and told his followers about all the burgers he flipped and dishes he washed while he was waiting to be signed then maybe the kids would pick up on it and work and learn while they wait for their rap star millions. Maybe.

I understand that it is a different world that our children are growing up in. It is much more complex. But understanding isn't forgiving or forgetting. And I refuse to let the world's complexity be used as an excuse for some of the shit that I witness on a daily basis

19

"If you have a dog, you will most likely outlive it; to get a dog is to open yourself to profound joy and, prospectively, to equally profound sadness."
                                            -*Marjorie Garber*

Unlike today, life was so much simpler when I was a kid. Children today need iPods, cell phones and $150 sneakers. All I needed was a dog, some gloves, a winter coat and a pair of waterproof boots and my weekend was set.

I was a child that loved being outside. When I think about my childhood I remember either being hot and itchy or cold and wet. When the weekend would arrive I would be up and out of the house early, especially if there was snow on the ground and a chance that the creeks and ponds would be frozen.

I would already be dressed, ready and wrapped up tight by the time my friends, Mark and Brian, arrived. They were two white brothers that lived about a mile away from us. Mark was two years older and Brian was my age and even in my class at school. Now that I am grown I can say that Mark was one of those kids that I wouldn't have wanted my kids to play with. He was respectful, smart and really good at fixing and rigging things. But just like Eddie Haskell, there was another side to him that showed up when there were no parents around.

From the fourth grade on up to whenever it was that girls came into the picture, I would spend my weekends, snow days and summer breaks navigating and exploring a five-square mile area around my house. I knew every stream, farmhouse, pond and path in or around Rectortown. The weather dictated our adventures. If it had just rained that meant the creeks and streams would be flooded, so we could have mile-long bottle races. The snow and freezing temperatures meant that we could risk our lives at *"The Pond with the Island"* chasing after the large mud turtles that were visible beneath the ice. We actually stood on the ice with sticks and rocks, cracking it, in order to scoot the turtle closer to the bank. How stupid we were. I am shocked that *"The Pond with the Island"* never swallowed one of us up. The summers were for miles and miles of bike rides, sneaking onto some stranger's property to fish their ponds, chasing birds with our BB guns and just plain old young boy mischief. It seems that most of the time my mother had no idea where I was. It contrasts so much with the way I am with my kids. I don't let them out of my sight.

One summer the three of us were jumping our bikes over a stream not far from my house. My bike ended up getting stuck in a deep area of the stream. I couldn't swim, plus it was my sister Joan's bike, so I was resigned to the fact that I would just have to walk home and argue with Joan later. I told you earlier that Mark had another side to him and on this day it reared its ugly head. He jumped into the water and pulled my sister's bike up to the road. He looked at me and said, *"Okay. There is your bike. Now you owe me, nigger."*

My fuse was a lot longer back then than it is now. I was ten and had never been called a nigger before. So it was a strange and almost time-lapsed moment that has stuck with me. I didn't even really understand how derogatory the word was at the time. I just knew that it was a word that white people were not supposed to use towards black people. I was stunned. I actually saw *"The Line"* as a ten year old. I wanted to make him bleed. But I didn't. I got on Joan's bike and rode home alone. The whole way all I heard was, "You owe me, nigger…nigger…nigger…nigger…**nigger…**

I wasn't exactly alone. I had Fifi with me. She was a Border Collie, my best friend and always by my side. *Oh and by the way, the next time I was called a nigger, it cost me three days off the school bus. And the last time a motherfucker called me a nigger, let's just say police officers and hospital visits were involved.*

As Fifi and I headed back home, I wondered if I should tell someone. I knew if I told my Uncle John he would take me back and make me fight Mark. I figured my mother would feel that way too. I was embarrassed. That is what I felt as I pedaled home. I rode home with my dog and I was the one with my tail tucked between my legs. I wasn't embarrassed because of what he said. I was embarrassed because he didn't have to suffer any consequences for what he said. I think that embarrassment and the fact that I never told anyone about it is what made me fight so hard the next two times I was called a nigger to my face. Repression is a painful bitch and I know two white boys that would wholeheartedly agree.

Mark wasn't all bad and he did come by later and apologize. I was young and more forgiving than I am now so it didn't take but a few seconds for things to go back to normal.

But I never forgot it and the episode made me realize, once again, that my dog was my only true friend.

My thinking is very old fashioned when it comes to certain things. One of those things is my belief that children need a dog. My mother must have felt the same way because throughout my childhood there were not many times that my family did not have at least one dog.

When I was younger, my mom worked at a restaurant in Middleburg, Virginia. One of the cooks used to give her a ride home in the evenings. He was a white guy and his name was Johnny. Ma was really fond of him and so were my sisters and I. He would always bring us something when he dropped my mother off. Usually it was candy, cakes or cookies. But one day he brought us a puppy. He was my favorite white person for sure after that.

I named the puppy Snoopy. He was a Border Collie and just as playful as ever. He was smart but also hard headed. For almost a year he followed me everywhere and would never listen when I told him to go back or stay. I remember that I was across the street in my Uncle Charles' yard jumping bikes over a ramp with Mark, Brian and William Brown. The ramp wasn't high enough to give us the desired jumping distance, so I crossed back over the street to get another cinderblock to increase the ramp height. I was barely up the embankment on the other side of the street before I could hear Snoopy's nails clicking on the pavement. I reached the top just in enough time to yell at Snoopy to go back. But of course he didn't listen and in almost an instant a car came flying around the curve and sped right over top of him. Right before my eyes. I heard a really loud pop as the car ran him down and I am guessing that was either his neck or back snapping. I stood there frozen and in disbelief. The lady that was driving tried to avoid Snoopy but I think the swerve is what got him. Snoopy was left lying in the middle of the street motionless. I knew he was dead.

I scrambled back down the embankment, ran into the street without looking and knelt down beside him. I could hear his breath and could tell that he was still alive. For a split second I wanted to yell, *"Someone call the ambulance!"* But I didn't. I just picked my dying friend up and out of the street and carried him home.

I carefully carried him to the front porch and screamed for my mother. She came to the door and saw that Snoopy wasn't moving.

"What happened to the damn dog, Marc?" She asked in a way that made me feel like she was blaming me.

"He got hit by a car." I said between my tears.

"How many times have I told you to stay out of the street? All day long crisscrossing back and forth across the road, you are lucky it wasn't you that got hit!" She fussed.

My mother was a good fusser.

I don't know when Snoopy died. It could have been as I carried him around the side of the house to the back porch. Or it could have been earlier or later. I don't know. I just know that whenever it was, I was with him. I laid his broken body down on the back porch right outside of my bedroom door and covered him with a green horse blanket and just sat there. My Uncle John would not be able to dig his grave until the next day, so I had to go to bed that night knowing that my dear friend was lying dead just outside the back door. It was not a good night.

Even though Snoopy was all that was on my mind that next morning, I didn't pull the blanket back on him. I didn't want to see him anymore. Not like that. I stayed away from the back porch all the way up until the hole was finished.

Snoopy's funeral was held the evening after his death and it didn't consist of hearses, flowers and preachers. It only consisted of me. The procession led from my grandmother's back porch, under the clothes line, down the field and over *"The Branch."* The funeral march did not stop until we were all alone at the bottom corner of our property. That little corner of our property was my family's very own pet cemetery. Chopper was the first that I can remember being buried there. He was our Great Dane and was taller than I was at the time he died. If Chopper didn't like someone that someone knew it. He didn't like Mr. Payne and went after him one day. The next morning while sitting at the kitchen table getting ready for breakfast, we looked out of the kitchen window and saw Chopper lying in the snow with his eyes open and tongue hanging out. My family still believes that Mr. Payne poisoned Chopper while we slept.

I was careful not to touch Snoopy as I picked up his lifeless body. I kept his face covered as I lifted him up off the back porch and not even a strand of hair from his tail was visible beneath the blanket. But covering him up didn't take him away. I knew what I was carrying. A friend.

His body was stiff and his legs stuck straight out. It was like carrying a large stuffed Scooby-Doo won at Kings Dominion. I walked down through the field and crossed over *"The Branch."* As I headed up to the corner where the grave was dug, I noticed that there was a mound of red dirt with a shovel sticking out of it.

I walked over to the edge of the hole and looked down into it. My Uncle John had laid blankets at the bottom of it. I was worried about that because even though Snoopy was heading back to from whence he came; I still didn't want his body on the ground. Strangely, I remember not wanting him to be cold. I got down on my knees and gently placed him in his grave.

"Bye Snoopy."

The first shovel full of dirt that I splashed over him felt and sounded wrong. So did the second, third and fourth but I managed to finish. And I made sure when I was done that his grave was perfect. There was no overgrown grass and extra dirt lying around the grave. It was as pristine as a fourth-grader could achieve and if it had of had a headstone it would have looked good enough to be a grave in a human cemetery.

I walked back towards the house with a gravedigger's shovel on my shoulder, Snoopy's collar in my hand and the sound of his neck snapping bouncing around in my head. Now that Snoopy was in the ground, my physical load was lighter but my emotional one was growing heavier with each step. And my back hurt. You don't realize how much space a dog takes up until it is gone. I skipped dinner and went to bed early that evening surrounded by so much emptiness that even the screams of the children playing right outside my bedroom window seemed miles away.

I woke up the next morning without my face being licked. I hated when Snoopy did that but on that morning I missed his cold wet nose like a new mother misses her baby on her first day back at work. I eventually ventured outside to find out what the day had in store for me. Nothing I found was enough to remove my friend from my thoughts. I remember that it was summertime when Snoopy died because it was still light outside when my mother and Johnny pulled up into the yard after work that day. My mother got out of the car with a huge grin on her face. It was a strange grin and let me know that she was giving something away.

It turns out that when my mother told Johnny about Snoopy's death and how sad we all were about it, he became really upset and decided to give us another puppy. Another Border Collie. Snoopy's sister from the same litter. Her name was Fifi.

I kept Fifi close. I was not going to lose this one. I got her back when I was in the fourth grade and she stayed with me all the way past graduation. A bond was built between us that I still feel to this day. I think the bond is still so strong because I lost her once before I lost her forever. I suffered through her death twice, literally.

Not long after giving us Fifi, Johnny got killed in a car accident. He was thrown from his car and it rolled over on top of him. My mother was really upset about it. Really upset. It was too bad because Johnny never got to see the lifelong friendship that he began.

Fifi and I quickly became inseparable. Like Snoopy, she was the type of dog that followed me wherever I went; even deep into the woods and across the street but she was smarter about it. She was more careful and almost seemed to look before she crossed the road. Sometimes I wonder if Snoopy warned her in her dreams the night before she came to us, *"You are going to the White's house in Rectortown? Sis, please, watch that curve, it's a doozie."* And as funny as it seems she did just that. I can remember Jean and especially Joan almost getting hit by a car more times than Fifi.

Fifi survived the curve in the road and together we had many adventures that lasted from grade school well past my high school graduation. She was a good dog and only bit one person, a mean bicycle throwing bitch that lived down the street. The lady reminded me of the Wicked Witch and had it coming if you ask me. But other than that we had no incidents. She never ran away. She never chewed up stuff. She didn't bark too much and when she did you knew to look.

Fifi avoided sickness all the way up until I was in the eleventh grade. That is when she started to scratch a lot. She was an indoor/outdoor kind of dog because we were indoor/outdoor kind of kids so it was not uncommon for me to pluck off a big fat tick from time to time. *I enjoyed hearing them pop as I smashed them between two rocks. I hope that doesn't make me a psychotic.* When her hair started to fall out in large clumps, I started to get nervous. We took her to the vet and they gave us some medicine to put in her food. It didn't work. And soon the bald areas on her back started to fill with raised blisters that oozed. I have to give it to Grandma, she spared no expense in trying to save Fifi for us, for me but nothing worked. We didn't know what was going on. The vet couldn't tell us anything. Fifi was weakening and she looked to be suffering. I knew the end was near for her.

Our church sent us to the Lott Carey Youth Seminar held at Shaw University in Raleigh, North Carolina. For my sisters and me, it was a time to have fun interacting and socializing with kids our age from up and down the east coast. For my grandmother it was the perfect time to put the dog to sleep.

I came home from Shaw and immediately noticed when I got out of the car that Fifi didn't come running to see me. I was ten feet from the car with bags in hand when Grandma came out of the front door. I wonder what was going through her mind when she got up that morning knowing that we were all coming home to a dead dog.

"Where is Fifi?" I asked the question to myself but I already knew the answer.

When she came outside and saw my eyes scanning the yard, Grandma didn't look at anyone but me and said, *"Marc, I had to put her to sleep."*

I dropped my bags and hit the road. I didn't know where I was headed; I just knew I didn't want to be there. I knew I didn't want everyone to see me cry. I was sixteen. I was tough and cool. I needed to be alone. I walked out of the driveway and headed up the street. I walked past the church. I walked past the corner. I walked past the basketball court and stopped at the school. I sat there alone on the front steps of my old elementary school and let the tears flow.

Time passed. Wounds began to heal. And life basically got back to normal. Well as normal as it could be considering the gaping hole that was left by the passing of my best friend.

It was summertime of 1987 when Grandma had Fifi put to sleep. Fast forward six or seven months to January 31, 1988. It was Super Bowl Sunday; my family was all crowded into my Aunt Sherry's house. The women were in the kitchen. The men were in front of the television. The game was on. The house was loud, the kids were running and jumping and no one cared because the Skins were winning. All of the sudden I heard my cousin Kameelah scream. Everyone ran into the kitchen to see what was going on and there outside the screen door was none other than Fifi. Alive. I hesitated for a minute because just like Kameelah, I thought I was seeing some ghost-like spiritual type shit and I was completely freaked out. Sherry opened the door and Fifi came rushing in to me. I remember thinking, *"She looks brand new."* All of her hair had grown back and the skin beneath it felt smooth and young. I couldn't understand what was going on. None of us could. But sure enough it was Fifi, live and in the flesh.

I have to admit, for a while I really thought that my dog had come back from the dead. I remember all of us grandkids running down the road from Sherry's house to Grandma's yelling and hollering because we were experiencing a miracle. It wasn't until Grandma called the vet that we found out what really happened. It seems that the vet had too big of a heart. When Grandma brought Fifi in to be put to sleep the doctor couldn't do it. He said that she still had so much life in her that it would have broken his heart to put her down. So instead, he nursed Fifi back to health. And he did a wonderful job at it. I don't know if he had intentions on keeping Fifi for himself or if he had plans on returning her to us. I guess Fifi didn't know either and she decided that she wasn't sticking around to find out. The first chance she got, she escaped and made her way home from many miles away. Yes, my family has its very own *Snoopy Come Home /Incredible Journey* story.

The vet was very apologetic when Grandma called him and felt awfully ashamed by what he had done but he received nothing but a massive amount of appreciation from her. Appreciation and many many *"Bless you's."* Unknowingly, the vet extended the friendship of a boy and his dog. That right there is special. He gave me my buddy back and that act alone had to earn him some Heaven Points.

The good doctor gave Fifi and I four more years together and we made the most of them. But she eventually got sick again. The same hair loss. The same blistery skin. Everything was the same except this time she was old. And this time, most importantly, I was prepared for her death.

It was like watching a movie that I had seen ten times before or reading a book again. I had been there before so I knew what each scene entailed and I knew how it was going to end. And when it did end, when she died, I remember that I wasn't as sad as I was the first time.

I experienced a similar feeling when my mother died. Just like with Fifi, I knew my mother was going to be leaving us soon. She stayed with me when she came home from the hospital and I had time to witness the downslide firsthand. And strangely, knowing what was coming seemed to ease the shock. Don't get me wrong, it was still my mama so the devastation was still there but the awareness that I had about what was coming made the collateral damage as minimal as could be considering the magnitude of the loss.

20

"Birth was the death of him."
-Samuel Beckett

I remember when I first thought that there might be something wrong with my mother. She was sitting on the sofa in the living room and I was in the kitchen folding clothes. It was morning but not early. I am guessing it was around 10:00AM or so. We were talking about where we were going to go for breakfast. All of the sudden she stopped talking. I thought that was odd so I walked into the living room and found her knocked out sleep. I was like, *"Ma!"* She snapped right out of it and looked very bewildered. I asked her if she was okay. She said she was fine but she just felt really tired. I asked her if she wanted to skip breakfast and she declined. So we get to the Waffle House and sit down to order. In the minutes that it took for us to figure out what the kids wanted to eat, Ma was asleep again. Inside the restaurant. I'm talking REM sleep. I knew something was wrong then. Once again, she snapped right out of it but she barely ate any of her food. After that episode I was on guard and so concerned that I barely ate any of my food as well. And I love Waffle House.

We got back to the house and I found myself staring at her. I'd watch her sit there and fight sleep like Deja and Desiree used to do while waiting for Santa Claus on Christmas Eve. Finally I could watch no more.

"Ma, I am calling the ambulance."

"No! Please Marc. I'm okay." She begged after snapping out of it.

I told her, *"Ma, you are scaring the shit out of me. You keep nodding off. Something is not right."*

"I'm just tired, Marc. Please. I don't want to go to the hospital. Please." **She pleaded.**

Not ten seconds after she said she didn't want to go to the hospital she was out again. That did it. I told Chrisi to call 911. When I snapped my mother out of her sleep and told her that the ambulance was on the way she cried.

She looked up at me with eyes that were filled with tears and fright and said, *"Marc, I'm scared."*

The ambulance came and the medics rushed into the living room and started doing their thing. Checking for blood pressure and oxygen levels. Strapping on the mask and hooking up the monitors. Feeling for this and listening for that. Their voices and actions seemed to infer that my mother was in pretty bad shape. They didn't say anything to me to let me know her status; it was just from observing their body language and voices that let me know that it was serious.

They rushed her out of the house and into the back of the ambulance. I hurried outside to tell her that I would meet her at the hospital. She was still crying. Everything was happening so fast that I didn't get the chance to worry. I mean I was worried. But not like a son should have been. I was busy being the *"Scene Handler"* and it wasn't until I was alone in my truck trailing behind the screaming ambulance that I processed the events of the day and first thought to myself, *"Ma is going to die soon."*

I parked my truck and speed walked to the Emergency Room. By the time I got to the room they already had her hooked up to all the monitors and stuff. She had a mask on but I could still see those fright filled eyes. I wanted to tell her that she was going to be fine but for some reason I have never been able to be that shoulder to cry on. I can't console and make people think everything is going to be alright. Especially when I know that things are not going to be alright.

The doctor came in and asked if he could speak with me outside. The outside part of the question is usually what lets people know that the news will not be good. But I knew from the moment she fell asleep over her bacon and eggs that the news would not be good. And it wasn't. If we had let my mother go to sleep that night, she would not have woken up. One of my babies could have found my mother dead. How awful a thought is that?

My mother had fluid around her heart. The fluid caused her heart to work harder than normal. That extra work led to the exhaustion and falling asleep. And finally, there it was - *possible death*. I am sick of those two words.

My mother's needs were too great for the local hospital so she was transported by helicopter to the Washington Hospital Center. There she was kept in a comatose state while air was forced into her lungs. For a while I didn't think my mother was walking out of that hospital. She stayed there for weeks while they tried to get her back in shape and for the bulk of that time she was completely out. I don't remember all of the medical details and terms but basically she was unable to breath through her normal airway and the doctors were forced to perform a tracheotomy. She was really depressed after that. I was disgusted and deeply saddened by that hole in my mother's throat and believe I hated it just as much as she did. But it was necessary to save her life and I just tried to look at it from that light.

As the days and weeks passed I watched as her prognosis got better each day. I am not saying that it wasn't a rough time. It was. On all of us. We were up and down the highway everyday and night. I was sick of that hospital. But she was getting better. I could see it. I had to suction the mucus from the hole in her neck. It was not something I was comfortable with, especially at first. *(Unfortunately, I inherited my mother's weak stomach and a lot of stuff makes me gag. A lot of stuff. Sometimes even the thought of or smell of some stuff.)* But thankfully, she got to the point where she could do it herself. Then soon after that she was able to get out of the bed and walk to the bathroom, then down the hall and then finally, out the door. Thank God.

She came to stay with me when she got out of the hospital and I have to admit it was a terrifying experience. She was constantly choking and coughing and there was always mucus everywhere. There were lots of times that I secretly questioned whether or not she was really ready to come home.

Being stuck in the hospital is probably a lot like being stuck in prison. All you think about is getting out, even if you are not prepared for life on the outside. And if you do find yourself out early then more often than not, you will find yourself right back in sooner more than later. That was the case with Ma. When she came home from the hospital there was episode after episode where we had to call the ambulance and watch them haul her off to the hospital to be strapped up to breathing equipment. We even had to call 911 on her birthday.

Since the doctors had to perform a tracheotomy on my mother, she couldn't talk. She had this device that covered up the hole in her neck and it was supposed to make her voice more clear. It didn't work well so we got her a bell. It was a really loud one that I still have. She used to ring it if she needed something. I could hear it even if I was outside.

Ma had been feeling really depressed in the days leading up to her birthday. And it was understandable. I would have hated to be in her position. She was loved and knew that she wasn't a burden but she wanted to go home. I hated having to talk to her about why I couldn't *"let"* her go home. But she understood. She knew that up the country where she lived, the ambulances couldn't get there as quickly as they could if she stayed with me. Minutes would matter if she had a serious episode. Why take the chance before you are absolutely sure you are ready? Plus she wouldn't have the kids around if she went back home. She loved my babies.

We wanted my mother's birthday to be a really happy event in the hopes that it would lift her spirits. We didn't tell Ma but we were cooking out and lots of family members were secretly coming over to the house to surprise her. Even my Aunt Francine was coming over and I knew Ma hadn't seen her in a long time. I knew she would be really excited at having Francine in the house. But even more, I knew she would be really happy in general just to have all of us around her on her birthday. That is what made the sound of that fucking bell so disgusting.

I was outside and across the parking lot at the playground with the kids when I heard the bell start ringing. It was ringing hard and loud and I knew it was not a, *"Marc, I need you to change the channel."* kind of ring. I scooped up the kids and sprinted as fast as I could back to the house.

All I could think as I raced across the parking lot was, *"Not on her birthday God. Please. This is supposed to be a good day."*

In the months that passed since my mother came home from the hospital there were many what I would call episodes and we would have to figure out if it was an episode that required a 911 call. Many nights we were able to work things out on our own with the oxygen masks and suction equipment that we had. But there were also many nights where we just had to call for help.

From the loud and constant ringing of that bell, I knew that the medics would have to be summoned this time.

Sure enough when I made it back to the house she was sitting there with that same panicked look on her face, in so much fear that she was bouncing up and down. She could hardly breathe even after I sucked out what looked like a gallon of mucus. I had to make the call.

Ma and the ambulance left about ten minutes before everyone started showing up. I decided that instead of following the ambulance to the hospital, again, I would finish cooking the food on the grill, wait until everyone got to the house, give them the bad news and then all of us make a trip up to the hospital together to see Ma.

In the couple of months that passed after my mother got out of the hospital, we had to call the ambulance to take her back several times. I could tell that she was tiring of the process and I worried that having to go to the hospital on her birthday might make her give up and throw in the towel. But she didn't and she came home from the hospital after a week or so and got better. A lot better. She was suctioning herself, doing her breathing treatments on time and even becoming slightly understandable when using that thing that helped her talk. She convinced me that she was well enough to go home. I knew it would at least pick her spirits up and decided to give it a go. It was one of those decisions that will haunt me forever. And after I dropped her and all of her medical equipment off at her house, all I could think about as I backed down her driveway was, *"This might be it."*

And I wasn't wrong. She wasn't home two weeks before she was dead.

In another of my favorite movies, *Saving Private Ryan*, Matt Damon had just found out that all of his brothers were killed in action. He told Tom Hanks that he could not see his dead brothers' faces when he thought about them. Tom Hanks told him that he had to think about his brothers in a context. He had to think about them in a moment. It works and the moment that I think about when I want to see my mother's face is her last birthday, the one in the hospital. When I think about that hospital room overflowing with grandkids and cousins and brothers and sisters laughing and singing Happy Birthday loud enough for the whole floor to hear, I see my mother's face clearly.

Location not withstanding it was one of those situations that I bet my mother, if she had survived her battle with congestive heart failure, would have looked back on as one of the most memorable moments in her life. But she had a new life waiting for her. So off she went.

Speaking of new life…

21

> ***"Birth is the sudden opening of a window, through which you look out upon a stupendous prospect. For what has happened? A miracle. You have exchanged nothing for the possibility of everything."***
>
> *-William MacNeile Dixon*

I have two sisters, a pair of twins that are a little over a year younger than me and they have both been two big pains in the ass from day one believe me. Seeing how my mother already came home with one little bastard child, Yours Truly, she kept her new pregnancy a secret. She didn't tell a soul and denied it fervently when asked. I know she must have been totally scared to death knowing that she was pregnant and once again without a baby's daddy. I am surprised that Grandma never figured it out. But she didn't and my mother's secret stayed intact.

As the due date neared and her girth became too much to conceal, my frightened twenty-three year old mother moved from up the country with her mother and father. She scooped me up and we landed at 53rd and E Street Southeast Washington DC. She moved us to the city to stay with her brother Howard and his wife Francine.

"Judy, are you pregnant?" my Uncle Howard asked when he first saw her.

"No I am not pregnant!" my mother lied.

"You look like you are pregnant." my Uncle Howard said suspiciously as he was on to her game.

On the night of February 13, 1973 my mother was up all night. She was back and forth to the bathroom. I was asleep in the room with my twin cousins Angela and Angeline. My mother's frequent trips to the bathroom woke my uncle up. My cousins Angeline and Angela are a few months older than me and we were all one and a half or so at the time so you can imagine the noise we would have made if we were awakened in the middle of the night, so my uncle tip-toed past our room. He knocked on the bathroom door and asked my mother if she was okay. She said she was a little sick, it was nothing; she just wasn't feeling too good.

My Uncle Howard went back to sleep and for the rest of the night all was good as far as he was concerned.

February 14, 1973. Valentines Day. My Aunt Francine is a nurse and that morning she got up early and headed off to the hospital. My Uncle Howard was going to school at the time and didn't have to be there until 10:00AM, so he slept in. Around 8:30AM my uncle was startled awake by my mother's bloodcurdling screams. He stumbled out of bed, ran to the bathroom, busted open the door and guess what he found on the floor?

A baby. Yuck.

My Uncle Howard ran to get a towel to wrap the baby up. It was a little girl. He told me that the whole house was screaming. He was screaming. My mother was in the bathroom sitting on the floor wailing. The new baby was also on the floor crying. Angeline, Angela and I were in our room each yelling and crying our eyes out. My Uncle Howard told me that there was snot everywhere.

My Uncle Howard ran to the phone and called Francine at work. He told her that my mother just had a baby in the bathroom. He hung the phone up and immediately sprinted out of the house. Screaming at the top of his lungs, he left a house full of kids, his sister in labor and what looked like a crime scene in his wake. He told me that he just panicked. He couldn't take it. The screams. The blood. The fact that there was a baby on the bathroom floor of his apartment. He couldn't wait. He decided he was going to run to Francine's job. As she was flying home as fast as she could from work, Francine drove past my uncle as he was running and screaming down the street like Richard Pryor on fire. She stopped and picked his crazy ass up. He was in a complete panic and totally out of breath. They rushed back to the house and she called the ambulance.

As the ambulance pulled off with my mother and the new baby, my uncle still could not get his shit together. He picked up the phone and called Grandma and Granddaddy in Virginia.

"Mama!! AAHHHHHHH!!! DADDY!! AAAAHHHH!!! Mama!! AAAAAHH!!! Judy!! Judy!!! AAAHHHH!!!! JUDY HAD A BABY!! AAAAHHHH!!!

Francine quickly snatched the phone from him. Thankfully because I am sure that Grandma was on the other end of the phone wondering what in the world was going on with my Uncle Howard and why he was hollering. My grandparents were very upset by the news and the way that they received it and came rushing from up the country to DC General Hospital where to everyone's surprise my mother had another baby. *"Great."* Another girl. My mother named the two babies Jean and Joan. The birth certificates say that Jean is the oldest. But my Uncle Howard says now and has always said that Joan was the one that he saw squirming around on the bathroom floor and I think he would know.

When my grandparents arrived at the hospital and found out that my mother had twins, they were just floored. They were worried and didn't know what to do. You have to remember that my mother was able to keep her pregnancy a secret the whole time, so in the span of an hour my grandparents didn't just learn that their daughter was pregnant. They learned that she was pregnant and had actually pushed the baby out already. And to top it off, while speeding down the highway still dealing with the shock of being kept in the dark about one child; they had to arrive at the hospital and learn that she had another baby. It was too much.

When the two black cats were finally out of the bag a decision had to be made. Ma couldn't take care of all of us on her own. Everyone knew that. A family meeting was held and when I say family meeting, I mean the whole family. Cousins, aunts, uncles, neighbors, everyone. I can't imagine how my mother must have felt sitting there in the middle of all of that with every eye on her. I am sure it looked like some sort of intervention or something. There were talks of putting Jean and Joan up for adoption but that was quickly ruled out. (Too bad I was too young to have my say.☺) Eventually, with the support of the whole family and neighborhood, a decision was made to keep the twins. After all, they were family.

Now I have two sisters who like I said are major pains in the ass and have been all my life. They fight. They always have. They argue. They always have. From the outside looking in, a stranger might think that they hate each other. But mess with one of them and watch what happens.

My sisters and I have a strange relationship. We all live within a mile and a half of each other. Everyone says that we are just like our mother. *"Y'all just like y'all mama. She moved to DC and didn't want to come back either."* I said that we all live a mile and a half from each other but really I live a mile and a half from them. They live on different sides of the parking lot in the same apartment complex.

If you ask me and remember I am their brother, they are both ghetto. The only difference is that Joan doesn't know it. She thinks she's classy.☺ We don't hug. We rarely ever say anything nice to each other. They use me for computer questions and repairs while I raid their refrigerators and use them to help get my kid's hair done. At the peak of her anger Joan will call us anything except our names. She has the uncanny ability to string derogatory words together like a fisherman's net. She likes to refer to me as *"Darkus," "Bucky," "Incomplete"* or simply *"an ugly motherfucker"* but she gets real creative when coming up with names for Jean. My favorite was when she called Jean *"a blue-lipped trick."* I still laugh about that one. My mother could cuss like that too. I think that is where Joan got it from.

It's funny but I don't think my sisters and I have ever told one another that we loved each other. I know we do but the thought of actually hearing the words from either of them or uttering them myself, seems almost unbearable to me. But I know that we do and because of them I don't have to ever worry about being homeless or hungry. I feel good knowing that my mother would be proud of the relationship that my sisters and I all have together. And with the end result in mind, I bet she would consider everything she went through in the bathroom that cold February morning absolutely worth it.

I have known for a while that I wanted to write about my sisters' birth. I was sure that I knew the story cold. My Uncle Howard has told the tale so many times over the years that I felt like I could write about it without even talking to him and I probably could have. But I thought it better to have a fresh picture of him running, palms up, down the street screaming and hollering before I could do the story any real justice. So I called him and asked him to tell me the story again. And again, I laughed out loud. I always do when he tells that story.

Jean and Joan's birth is one of those stories that I can't wait for my kids to be old enough so I can laugh with them about it. They are going to get a huge kick out of it. You might say, *"Why wait?"* It is simple to me. They are ten and eleven. I don't think the kids need to know everything now. I believe that innocence is golden and should be held onto.

22

> *"Always end the name of your child with a vowel, so that when you yell the name will carry."*
>
> *-Bill Cosby*

I am very selective about what I divulge to my kids, especially when it comes to my past. Please understand that I am not embarrassed of my past and I want the kids to learn from it. But they are still children and I am in no rush for them to grow up. But they are. And fast. Their growth makes me feel the need to grow. I want them to be proud of me.

One time I heard NBA All-Star Allen Iverson respond to a question about the change in his attitude and behavior. He said, *"My kids are old enough to read the newspapers now."* I know exactly what he was talking about because gone are the days when I could spell out the words I didn't want the kids to hear me say. Whoever said, *"They grow up so fast."* hit the nail on the head. I have watched my children grow from tiny little infants into big girls that can almost look me dead in the face and I'm 6'3".

I don't know if I am trying to keep things from them for selfish reasons or what especially considering how fast the world is. It seems like all the little girls that my kids grew up watching on TV are in and out of rehab or showing their asses and other private areas to the paparazzi. My kids and I haven't had the *"Birds and the Bee's"* talk yet, largely because I am scared to death of having it but I am sure they have ideas. *AAAAHHHH!!!!"*

Why can't they stay kids forever? Why do boys and periods and bras have to come into the picture? There is actually going to come a time when I am going to find a tampon or maxi-pad wrapper in my bathroom trash can. Do you have any idea how frightening that thought is? Those wrappers are going to make me really miss the good old days when all I had to look forward to in the bathroom was a pair of underwear with *"poop 'tains"* in them or a toilet seat covered with *"brown stuff."*

One time not too long ago I walked into my bathroom and was frightened by what I saw. Actually, terrified would be a better word. I rushed out of the bathroom to examine my kids because from the look of the toilet seat one of them was very sick.

"Deja! Are you okay?" I asked with all the concern of a loving father.

She looked at me like I was crazy and said, *"Yeah."*

"Desiree, baby are you okay?"

She hardly looked up from her Wii Bowling game and said, *"Yeah Daddy."*

"Ok! Pause the damn game!" I said loudly and standing in front of the television .with a serious look on my face.

"Desiree, you're okay? You're sure?" I asked again.

Again I got the same response from her. *"Yes Daddy, I am fine. Come on, I was close to my high score."*

"Deja, you are not sick?" I asked her again as well.

She responded, *"No Daddy. Why do you keep asking us that?"*

Finally I said, *"I keep asking because it looks like someone's ass exploded on my toilet seat!"*

They both busted out laughing.

I said, *"Stop the damn game and come here!"* And I dragged them both to the bathroom to make sure they could see what I was seeing.

To me, the toilet seat and bowl looked like it could have been in a Midwest truck stop somewhere.

"If neither one of you are sick then what the hell is all of that brown stuff on my toilet seat?"

Desiree peeked into the bathroom and simply said, *"Ew. That's not my mess."*

We both turned to Deja. She looked up at me and said, *"My bad, Daddy."*

I was like, *"My bad? What the hell you mean my bad? Why is there shit all over my toilet seat?"*

They were really cracking up then. It seems they love to see me bewildered. But I needed answers and I needed them immediately. *"Deja, what is all over my toilet seat?"*

Deja said, *"It's chocolate, Daddy. I tried one of those chocolate covered cherries that you brought home from work. It was nasty so I spit it out and it went all over the toilet seat."*

I asked her. *"Why didn't you clean it up?"*

She looked at me and I flashed back to when she was a little baby. She said, *"I tried but it wouldn't come off."*

I actually felt sorry for her for a second. Then I told her, *"Well there is some Comet under the kitchen sink. Get to scrubbin' because looking at that mess is making me gag."*

One of the many things that I love about my kids is that they are still *"kids."* They show no interest in boys, they pluck the cookie dough chunks out of the ice cream; they leave the bathtub slippery, spill stuff and make messes. Kid stuff. They are not rushing to grow up like a lot of the little girls that I see everyday. I am happy about that and I do my part to make sure growing up is not a speedy and overnight thing for them. For example, Deja asked me the other day if she could read my first book. I thought about all of those cuss words and immediately said, *"No, baby. You are not old enough."* Don't get me wrong, my kids hear me cuss. It isn't something that I do often around them and it isn't anything I am proud of but sometimes they seem to just pull the filth from my mouth. I don't worry about it too much because my kids for the most part do as I say not as I do. But I felt that by allowing Deja to read my book, I would be exposing her to a lot of feelings and emotions that she just wasn't ready for.

Let me say this. I am not proud of the language I used a bit excessively in my first book. In fact I am a bit ashamed. But those feelings are mine and mine alone. Let me grow as a writer, will you? First of all, I write for me. I don't write for the preachers and church ladies and yet I have had both tell me that they loved my book. If you remember me as Mattie White's little angel of a grandson, that is fine. But I am a man now, my wings are long gone and I am not changing for you.

It seems that the closer people get to death the closer they try to get to God. And for some reason they always try to take me with them. I find it funny. And I mean funny ha ha. And I am laughing because I see the hypocrisy. *"I would feel more comfortable telling people about your book if it didn't have so many cuss words in it. You know people remember you as Mattie White's good little boy?"* That is what I hear now. And I usually hear it from people that I've heard cuss. From people that I have personally seen running like the wind. Why be fake? Why pretend you don't cuss because you go to church? Why not be happy for Mattie White's little grandson that in spite of everything in his path he still grew up to be a fairly decent young man and an author of two good books? Haters and Fakers, the world is full of them.

Have you ever read an email or letter that you took the wrong way? Sure you have. Most people don't talk the way they write and even if they do it still does not come across the same. That is why all of those instant messaging programs come with smiley faces and other *"emoticons"* to let people know on the other end that you are happy, laughing, mad, etc. There are inflections, variations and intonations in your voice that allow people to know how you feel about what you are saying. Also there are facial expressions and hand gestures that all help to let people know what you are feeling as you talk.

Problem is people can't hear or see me when I write so what better way is there to let a reader know I am angry than a cuss word? My cuss words came from emotion and repression. I was a different person when I wrote my first book. I always considered myself a private person and there I was spilling my guts and putting it on paper. I didn't know what I was doing. I was a rookie writer that was going through a traumatic metamorphic process. I wasn't writing a book, I was suffering and a book was just a by-product of it. I was changing and if change was the message in my first book, I guess growth is the message for this one. And because of that I purposely monitored my language in this book. I monitored my language not because I don't cuss, because I do. Not because people told me to, because I don't care. I did it because I am writing this book with my kids in mind and I write it wanting them to read it. I want them to learn from the lessons that writing has taught me. The main one is say what you feel but be very careful if you write those feelings down because everyone is not going to get it. Everyone is not going to follow your flow. Words can be misunderstood and misconstrued even when spoken but when you write them down in a book, they are there to be misunderstood and misconstrued forever.

That is just one of the many lessons and instructions I try to pass on to my kids. They go to a really good school and I also try to impress on them to take advantage of their educational opportunities because there are so many that would love to be in their position. They are ten and eleven and I already feel like I am running out of time to leave an impression on them. As they get older I find myself reluctantly rehearsing my off to college or *"leaving the nest"* speech. It needs some work.

I don't preach college to my kids. I know some might consider that stupid. Don't get me wrong, I plan on supporting my babies with their decisions and steering them in the right direction. And if they decide that college is what they want to do then I will be right there beside them. No question. But to me, a college degree doesn't carry the weight that it once did. When I was growing up and before, a college degree almost guaranteed a good job and promising future. That was back when it was harder to get one. Back when blacks had to break tackles and make free throws to get one. But now that every Tom, Dick and Sheniqua has a degree it doesn't mean as much in the workplace or to me and I feel that looking inside yourself for a way to survive and provide should be just as high up on the list as Georgetown.

If your dream is to be a fashion designer, why go to college for four years, spend two of those years in a classroom studying English and Calculus and then start your adult life off with so much debt when all you want to do is sew and draw? Makes no *cents* to me. We all have talents. For some of us it is hard to dig them out of their shell.

But when you find it and see that there is a potential for success. You just have to go for it and you are crazy if you don't.

My humility makes separating myself from the rest of society very difficult. I don't like to consider myself special. But technically I am. Being special puts me in a smaller group of people. All that you have to do to be a member of that group is have the ability to do something that everyone else can't. Whether it is gliding from the free throw line and dunking the ball, raising good kids or writing a book. *(I mean a good book. Any Moe with a couple hundred dollars, some free time and a word processor can write a book nowadays.)* For my daughter Deja, what will guarantee her place in the group is softball and pitching. I know it. We've gotten to the point now that opposing coaches complain that she pitches too fast and it scares their girls. How awesome is that? We haven't quite put our finger on Desiree yet but she is just like her Daddy so I don't worry too much about her finding her way and getting everything in life that she wants.

23

"In the confrontation between the stream and the rock, the stream always wins - not through strength but by perseverance."

-H. Jackson Brown

New Car: $18795

Plane ticket to Boston to pick up new car: $232

Speeding ticket 30 minutes after leaving the car dealership: $190

Washington DC Excise Tax: $1295

Gas Prices: Highe$t on Record

No more waiting for Metro trains and buses: PRICELESS!!!

Yes sir, Marcus White just bought a new automobile. A Cadillac, which to me is the Cadillac of all automobiles. I love the song and play it often but I chose not to *throw some d'z on that bitch* simply because I'm grown. It is not a new car but it is new to me and I treat her like she just rolled off the showroom floor. Seriously, the car is a big deal though and I feel like a major goal has been met because if you know me then you know that all I wanted was a Cadillac. I guess I am fitting the stereotype but all of my life I have done that so oh well.

I admit that my fascination with Cadillac automobiles could be a black man thing but it is just something about the sharp angles of the exterior and the way the right color can perfectly accentuate the headlights. The smell of the leather is more pleasing to me than a bouquet of fresh cut wildflowers. And the heated seats, oh Desiree and I just love the heated seats. I'm totally infatuated with the comfort, the handling, the power and the glory forever and ever. Amen. I watch the Cadillac commercials, where Tiki Barber and other celebrities talk about how much they love their Cadillac and think to myself, *"I could do that, easily."* Especially when I am driving through the 3rd St. Tunnel.

Honestly I feel that I can do whatever I set my mind to. I get what I want and I do not settle. A Cadillac was just one of the many goals that I have set for myself and it feels good to cross it off. But my list is still long and growing. My new car was a positive step forward, yes but nothing good seems to come to me without being followed closely by something bad.

The problem that my step forward has caused is the way people look at me now. Basically, you can't dap up everyone in the hood. Some just get a *"What's up?"* or a head nod. That being said, it is still your neighborhood and like it or not you become known because the hood is nosy and sooner or later your business is going to get out. And when you keep to yourself and are not loud with your shit, people in the hood wonder about you. They assume.

My Cadillac was a goal. One set years ago. It didn't seem odd to me to want something and then work towards it. But from the looks of things the idea of setting *"realistic"* goals seems to be a foreign concept in the hood. And that fact was made clear to me immediately after I parked that shiny gold Cadillac in the parking lot of my apartment building.

To those that don't understand me or the strength of my desire, I went from standing at the bus stop in the hood to driving a Caddy overnight. But those that do understand my commitment to reaching my goals know that I walked, caught the bus and train, missed out on a lot of stuff and inconvenienced a lot of people for over two years while I waited for the ability to get my Cadillac. I didn't go the two years without a car because I couldn't afford one. I didn't walk so much that I need surgery on both feet because I liked to stop and smell the roses. I did all of that for two years for one reason. I wanted a Cadillac and I was not going to settle for less. But some see my baby step forward as a giant leap.

I am still trying to figure out the thought process of the people in my neighborhood as I am still relatively new here. But from what I can tell, in the hood, a new Cadillac means that you either hit a number or received an inheritance. It does not mean that you scraped and cheaped and grinded your ass off to get your credit report straight. No it could never mean that. In the hood when someone is seen driving a Benz or some other luxury car, people automatically assume, *"Oh, he must have money."* I on the other hand, assume something totally different and I bet I am more close to the driver of the nice car's reality. When I see that man park his Benz in the hood, I see a man that got something he wanted. I see a man with a car note, insurance premiums, registration fees, title fees and excise tax charges. What I don't see is a man with money, at least not with money to spare.

There needs to be an attitude adjustment in the hood from what I can see. I'm no social worker or psychologist and my observations and assessments come strictly from riding the train and bus. From walking the dog around the block. From living here.

There are not enough plans being made. Not enough realistic dreams being had and goals being set. You have to set goals. You have to write them down and tell people what they are even if they laugh at you. Otherwise you stay put. For instance, one day I plan on owning a Cadillac Sixteen. Yeah, baby! Yeah!

I just don't get it because it almost seems like the obvious is undetected. When I speak of the *"obvious"* I am talking about that slow train that is chugging its way through the hood gobbling up poor people's homes and leaving behind stadiums, bars, hotels and condos that most in the hood will never be able to afford. Bob Dylan sang, *"...the enemy I see wears a cloak of decency."* What I take his words to mean is that the people that claim to be doing what is best for us are the ones that really have us on their minds the least. Sometimes I can't believe the audacity it takes to build a huge four-hundred thousand dollar home and place it right next to a flop house where the drunks and crackheads live. They dangle that brand new shit over our heads like carrots and at the same time let our old apartments deteriorate beneath our feet until we can't take it anymore and move out. Then, when the building is empty, that is when all the money that was never used on us is then used to renovate and develop our broke down apartments into new and expensive condominiums. I tell people all the time that in ten years, living in Southeast is going to be totally different experience. An experience filled with a whole lot less poor black people.

I watched daily for over the last few months as a group of Hispanics built two big townhouses on the next street over. I am not in a rush to try to buy a house but I have been keeping my eyes open. When I saw those houses coming up I just knew that, considering the location and the average income of the people living in the neighborhood that the houses would be in the $250,000 range. A lot of money, yes but still within the amount of what I would probably look to spend when I am ready. And worth it because they were really nice houses.

They had an Open House the other day and I walked over to check it out. The front door looked like it should be on a house in Hollywood somewhere. The hardwood floors shimmered with a mahogany that was so deep that it looked like candy. I told the lady that answered the door, *"Okay, this house is way too pretty. Tell me how much it costs before I step another foot inside this door."*

A very polite and middle-aged black lady answered, "$386,000."

I said, *"Goodbye."* And turned to head back down the steps.

I am determined to beat that slow train to the station. I feel like I am not just fighting for my own future and security. I am fighting and struggling for a successful future for my kids as well. I don't contribute to any form of retirement or 401K. I need all of my money now. I have almost mastered the art of living check to check. Therefore I have to make it with my writing. I am beginning to be confident enough in my skills to believe that my goal of becoming a successful writer is almost within reach. I just have to keep pressing on. And I do. It has only taken me a quarter of the time to write this book that it took me to write my first one. And honestly I am more proud of this one. I feel the need for speed. I want to be ready with a second book in hand when that email, phone call or knock at the door comes and tells me that I made it.

I've written up an email that I saved and send out to hundreds of strangers each week introducing myself and telling them a little about my book. I do that in the hopes that somehow someone might get my book into the hands of someone that can help me.

Oprah, are you listening?

I have received a lot of replies and words of encouragement but nothing life changing yet. Prison gave me patience and even though my mind is racing, I can wait, at least for a little while longer. But the truth be known, I got to get out of here. I am better than this. I know it. I have made that statement to a lot of people. *"I am better than this. There is more for me out there."* It is not a feeling of cockiness or overconfidence. It is just something that I have always felt inside. Even when I was locked up, I knew there was more in store. I have always felt like I wasn't ready but I finally feel like I am. I've been walking around so much that my feet hurt. It is time to spread my wings. Fly a little. So let's get on with it and do the damn thing.

24

"Talent alone cannot make a writer. There must be a man behind the book; a personality which, by birth and quality, is pledged to the doctrines there set forth and which exists to see and state things so and not otherwise."
-Ralph Waldo Emerson

In the book business I have learned that it is not what you know or what you can do; it is more who you know and what they can do for you. Unfortunately, you definitely need help in this business. That fact makes success harder for me because that is one thing that I hate asking for. Therefore I keep grinding it out on my own with my hopes and dreams steering my ship into to the darkness of the unknown.

Lately I have found myself at a crossroad. I have been wondering if my lack of success with my book has really just been a lack of commitment. My job at the home has been a wonderful, warm and comfortable security blanket. But I wonder if its *"Linus Effect"* is holding me back. I'm not motivated to get out there and pump my book like I would be if I *needed* to be out there pumping my book. I'm not motivated because I have a great job that pays me enough to not have to worry about being homeless or hungry. But what if I were? Worried about being homeless of hungry, I mean. Then what? Then how many Metro Stations and office buildings would I be sitting in front of with a stack of books?

I am seriously considering pushing all of my chips to the center of the table, quit my job and just go for it. I feel that together my books are a good product and people have made millions off of a lot less. I just need to get my books into the right hands and let my writing speak for itself. That means the struggle continues. But I am down for it.

I was watching LOVE TV, a local television station that allows young wanna-be rappers the chance to rock the mic in front of the camera. It is very amusing television I must say and yet at the same time kind of sad. But anyway, one of the rappers being interviewed made a statement that I agree with completely. He said, *"You have to be accepted in the hood before you can make it nationally or worldwide. The hood has to give you the green light."*

The problem with getting green lit from the hood is that there doesn't seem to be too many readers around and the ones that I do find seem to lose interest after I tell them my book costs fifteen dollars. That really bothers me because I thought long and hard about setting the price of my book. I didn't want to seem greedy and yet at the same time I wanted to use my book as a way to better myself financially. After all, my book is about my life; it is no fairy tale filled with made up names and places. This shit really happened to me and my family. I am giving you a piece of my life for fifteen bucks. That is a steal if you ask me.

There have been times when I churned out six chapters in a week. Then I can turn right around and not write a sentence for over a month. Not because I didn't have anything to say. I always have something to say. It was more because I need my feelings to come across clearly and if I'm not in the *"mood"* to write then I feel like I am forcing it and somehow fake. For me, writing is not what I would call fun. Not this kind of writing. Poems are fun. But writing my books have been downright painful. Writing them has been a physical and emotional rollercoaster ride of feelings that takes me up and down the tracks with the ferocity of The Rebel Yell. I have to relive a lot of bad days and then after I intentionally immerse myself in a dreaded past I then have to figure out how to describe what I witnessed and felt in a way that readers will find entertaining. I seem to be good at it so I have to push on but it is still work and like I said well worth fifteen dollars. The part that really bugs me is that if I were on the train or in front of the grocery store selling CD's and DVD's, I would be rich by now.

On top of the value that I place on the reality of my writing there is also, like I said, the suffering that my writing brings along with it. The agony that I intentionally put myself through in order to give you the reader, a real and honest insight into my world requires a great deal of effort. I don't just sit down and write. My sentences don't just magically appear out of thin air. For me, writing is almost an out of body experience. Sometimes I feel almost like I have to die and then resuscitate myself in a time gone by where dead people that I love are still alive. I have to do that in order to give the most accurate description of events and my feelings concerning them. People say all the time that when they read my book it is almost like they can hear me talking, like I am reading it to them. That is the compliment on my writing that I like receiving the most. That and when people tell me that they can feel my emotions when they read my words. Those two accolades validate my writing and make all of the pain and suffering of the struggle worth it.

The former Black Panther, Fred Hampton, said in the months before he was killed, *"If you dare to struggle you dare to win. If you dare not to struggle. Then god dammit you don't deserve to win!"* I think the struggle makes me want it more. I know it makes me a better writer. But what if I didn't have it? The struggle I mean. Some people need adversity in order to be great. Some need to have that just out of reach goal just to have a reason to get out of bed in the morning. I think I am one of those people.

You don't know where the line is until you cross it and in my time I have left enough lines in my wake to re-chalk FedEx Field. I am not trying to be a role model and even though to a degree I am considered a success story by my peers, I still don't feel like the person to listen to when you need help with life-changing decisions. But if you are going to learn anything from me then learn to build your ark before the rainstorms come. Preparation. I have been so used to sloshing around in the rain and mud trying to get my act together that I lost focus on how to reach my full potential. Now things are different. Now I am different. Now I am more focused. Now I prepare. Now I am ready. I am a writer.

I really like how I ended that last paragraph. *"I am a writer."* That's what's called a power statement. But what's funny is that I have written two books, worked in front of thousands of computers and yet I still have to look at the keys when I type. Some writer I am. Huh? My 11th grade typing teacher Mrs. Pilla would be so ashamed of me.

I am very proud of this book and I think that is because it is real. Somehow I have squeezed two books out of one life. These words are mine. My books are me. And that is why I didn't succumb to the pressure and put everyone's name in it. In my eyes, doing that would be fake. And I just can't do it. I won't do it. *"How come she made it into the book and I didn't?"* or *"What you gonna write about me?"* To me that takes a lot of nerve to stand in my face and ask me that. My kids didn't even get mentioned in my first book. And there are many people that I love that didn't get mentioned in either of my books and it wasn't because I didn't love them. It was because, for whatever reason, they didn't fit with the flow of my stories not that they weren't important people in my life. If I am going to write about every conversation I have throughout the day I would never get a book finished. Hell, why even write? I can just walk around with a video camera all day.

I'm trying to do something here. I'm trying to take the puzzle pieces of my life and turn them into perfect *"paragraphical"* photographs. Everything has to fit. Everything has to flow. I'm a Libra. We are like that. My memory is like a black bag full of computer screws dumped onto the dining room table. Some are always going to fall onto the floor. Meaning that some are going to get left out of that specific computer. That doesn't mean they are gone forever or meaningless but it also doesn't mean the computer will not get built without them. Because of them I know where to look when I need a screw for the next computer that comes through the door needing repair. This second book right here is filled with screws that fell off the table when I was writing my first one. So all I can say to those that are wondering why their names were not mentioned here in this book is, *"I hope the vacuum cleaner doesn't get you."*

You can't tell me what to write. You can't advise or lead me. That doesn't work. I write from listening to people. From watching people. From walking the dog. I never know what is going to make a memory or thought pop into my head as I get all of my inspiration simply from living my life.

A while back I was facing some time in jail. Shocker, I know. It was only going to be for two weeks or so but those two weeks were really going to cost me. The closer the court date got the more and more stressed I got. I didn't know what to do.

I decided to put my writing skills to the ultimate test and I sat down in front of the computer and typed up a letter to the Commonwealth's Attorney that was handling my case. It was a last ditch effort and my chances of escape were slim but I was out of ideas.

In my letter I told her about my past. I told her about my hopes for the future. I told her about my first book that I was still writing at the time. I told her about my kids. I explained to her just how much two weeks in jail would cost me. In words I let that lady know exactly what was at stake for me. I basically pleaded for my life. I needed her to see me as a person not just another name on the docket. I put the letter in the mail not knowing what would come of it and when my court date arrived I was prepared for the worst.

I sent the dog to go stay with the kids. I parked my car in the first parking spot and asked my neighbor Miss Theresa to keep an eye on it for me. In the days leading up to my court date I told my boss that I was going to have to take some time off for personal reasons, I wasn't sure if that was going to work or not but it was all I had and it wasn't a lie. When it was finally time to go I emptied my pockets of everything except keys and change for the bus and train, took off my chain, made sure that all the lights were off and the iron unplugged, locked the door and headed off to jail.

I arrived at the court house on time and headed upstairs. I took a seat in the waiting area and, well, waited. I waited for minutes that seemed like hours. I can't explain it but time seems to slow down tremendously when you are sitting in a court house. Especially when you already know that you are not leaving that court house without handcuffs on.

My lawyer showed up and said, *"I have some good news and bad news."*

"Give me the bad news." I said almost ready to hear her say, *"They are seeking the Death Penalty for finding that blunt in your car."*

She said, *"Our judge is not in a good mood this morning. He was called in at the last minute and is not happy about it"*

"Well that is bad news." I said. "Especially since I haven't gone in front of him yet. What's the good news?"

She smiled and said, "The good news is that they are willing to drop your sentence from twenty days to ten."

I said, "That means I only have to do five days in jail."

"It sure does." She said.

"Well that is really good news." I said without trying to conceal my enthusiasm.

When my name was finally called I eagerly stood up, walked down the aisle and faced the judge. My charges were read and the judge asked the Commonwealth's Attorney for her recommendation. She said, "We are asking for five days and a fine of $250, Your Honor."

I was stunned. I asked myself if I heard her correctly, "Did she just say "five" days?

She did and the judge accepted her recommendation. That meant that I would only have to serve three days, two and some change if I got booked fast enough. I was siced. Before the cops led me away I got a quick moment to speak to the Commonwealth's Attorney. I thanked her graciously and told her, "You have no idea what you just did for me."

She stopped packing up her brief case, looked me straight in my face and said, "It was your letter that did it. You get your act together and keep on writing."

I haven't stopped.

When I was finishing up my first book I knew that there would be another one at some point. I set a goal of three. I had planned to take the easy way out and do a hard-cover revised edition of my first book maybe include some pictures and get rid of a lot of those cuss words. But the more I thought about it, I decided to leave my first book alone. I need people to read my first book in its original and raw state in order to see the growth and maturity that I feel is shown here in my second.

Book Number Three is going to be a problem though because as I sit here now I have nothing planned, nothing scrambling around inside this egg of a head I have. That concerns me a little. I spoke in a previous chapter about what I believe happens when you complete your *"task."* I'm wondering if I am completing my *"task"* as I am completing this book. I said earlier, *"...every single keystroke fulfills my destiny."* I know what that means. It might be getting close to check out time. But I'm not going to worry myself about that. Not too much, anyway. I'm going to keep on typing and wherever my words lead me I will follow, even if it is to my grave.

CPSIA information can be obtained at www.ICGtesting.com
223734LV00003BA/5/P